# Hope The Dude Can Play
## Lost Jimi Hendrix guitar rediscovered by GenZ player

By James Vasey
(Inspired by an actual event)

*Hope the Dude Can Play* is a work of fiction inspired by an actual event. Most of the characters are fictional. Any actual persons, living or dead, were depicted with the utmost respect. It is not meant to be an accurate account of the incident but purely for entertainment purposes. The truth lies somewhere in the Strato-sphere.

Copyright © 2024 by James Vasey All rights reserved.

No portion of this book may be reproduced in any form without written permission from the publisher or author, except as permitted by U.S. copyright law.

ISBN: 9798884204539

**Cover Photograph:**
The photo used in the cover graphic was taken by Ian Wright for *The Northern Echo* on February 2nd, 1967, the day of the Jimi Hendrix Experience concert in Darlington, and is published with the kind permission of the newspaper.

**Cover design:** Mike Brough at Fusion Creative

**Editor:** Steve Lockley

**Interior formatter:** Diane Kane

## Dedication

To the people of Darlington.

It seems perverse that York celebrates highwayman, Dick Turpin and Nottingham their prince of thieves, Robin Hood. So why not Darlington's infamous thief of Jimi's favourite Stratocaster?

Of all Darlington's connections to global fame—Robert Stephenson, Edward Pease, Sir Edmund Backhouse, and Lewis Carroll—townspeople tell the Jimi Hendrix tale with the most glee.

Arguably, the world's most famous guitarist would later mix with a million people in the chaos of the Isle of White Festival and Woodstock without losing a single instrument. And yet, legend would have us believe that among just 200 of Darlington's (mostly) good people, one of them stole his guitar—or did they?

### Jimi Hendrix

- Born Johnny Allen Hendrix; November 27, 1942, Seattle, Washington, USA
- Arrived in London, an unknown musician, on October 1$^{st}$, 1966, and changed his name to Jimi.
- By then, the world's highest-paid rock musician, Jimi headlined at Woodstock on 18$^{th}$ August 1969.
- Jimi died at The Samarkand Hotel, Borough of Kensington and Chelsea, London September 18th, 1970.

## Origin Of the Title

On 2nd February 1967, The Jimi Hendrix Experience appeared before fewer than 200 people at an R&B club in Darlington.

*"After the show, a black Fender Stratocaster belonging to Hendrix is said to have been stolen. Some say it was taken from the back of the tour van, others that it was nicked from the stage. Legend has it that, upon hearing the news, Hendrix said: "I hope the dude can play." Chris Lloyd, The Northern Echo, January 28th, 2017*

What became known as the Darlington Stratocaster has never been found.

2017 50th Anniversary Review by Chris Lloyd reproduced with the kind permission of The Northern Echo.

*The Imperial Hotel at the corner of Grange Road and Coniscliffe Road, close to the centre of Darlington, 1960s*

*The Imperial building today with Manjaros occupying the space where Jimi Hendrix played.*

**The Imperial Hotel**

The Imperial Hotel stands at the busy corner of Grange Road and Coniscliffe Road, close to the centre of Darlington. The impressive façade and entrance of the brick and sandstone Victorian building have changed little since its opening, although the use of the building is very different today. The former hotel is currently divided into office space with bars and independent restaurants on the ground floor.

When Jimi Hendrix appeared at The Imperial it was still operating as a residential hotel, with a ballroom, and cellar bar open to the public. The Darlington R&B club met there each Thursday during the sixties, and it was a popular place for fashionable young people to meet for a drink. The room where Jimi played is currently one of a chain of Afro-Caribbean restaurants called Manjaros.

Several people who attended the gig report seeing, and even speaking to Jimi afterwards in what was then the basement Bolivar. Today it is called Joe's - but should surely be Hey Joe's.

# Jimi aims to be as original as can be

ALLENE JAMES

THE Imperial Hotel, Darlington, home of the popular R and B club, really began to vibrate the night Jimi Hendrix came to town, and what a reception he got from the members!

About 200 young people stopped dancing and crowded around the platform to see the man himself at work. One couldn't deny that this artiste is a colourful one, both in his dress and comments, and in an interview after his performance he told me:

"The group and I have only been together since September, and yeah man, we're pretty happy about our present position in the charts." Fans will be pleased to hear that an L.P. album is soon to be issued, but I gather they are likely to release another single first.

Jimi thinks that there is a lot of copying in the pop world, and said: "We like to be original, and quite honestly each time we play it's different from the last. One never quite knows what will come out."

I asked him why he spelled his name Jimi, and not the usual way. "Well, I guess there's millions of Jimmy Hendrix's in America so I thought I'd be different. When I was a kid I wanted to be a movie-star or a cowboy — I suppose all American boys do — but then music began to get a grip on me, and here I am."

A fond traveller, Jimi is looking forward to trips to Belgium, Holland and Sweden in the near future. His last message to his Darlington fans was: "We like the audiences up here. They're very critical, but at least they listen. Oh yeah, we hope to be back!" And if the 200 R and B addicts were anything to go by, they'll no doubt echo that sentiment.

★ ★ ★

I ATTENDED a marvellous effort by young people and youth leaders, in the centre of Barnard Castle last weekend, when members of the Inter-Church Youth Club staged a full day's outdoor entertainment, and kept two stalls going with an inexhaustable supply of goods, to raise funds for "senior citizens to go on holiday."

The club staged a centre-of-town three-wheeler tricycle race, and Jane Grier, 16, spent most of the day being pushed around town in a wheelbarrow, by Adrian Bradley, of the RAPC at Deerbolt Camp, and shaking collecting tins at passers-by.

Jane has just moved to the area from Leeds, and she told me: "It's been very good, and great fun. The local people have responded very well indeed, and have been most generous." Adrian agreed. "I've seen this kind of thing done in London before, so we tried the idea here. It's gone far better than we expected, and although our original aim was to send two elderly people on holiday, we may be able to send more now."

*Interview with Jimi Hendrix by journalist Alene James, 2nd February 1967, reproduced with the kind permission of The Northern Echo.*

**The Jimi Hendrix Experience**

Jimi Hendrix arrived in the UK as an American solo artist in September 1966. Only when British musicians Noel Redding (right of centre) and Mitch Mitchell (left) were recruited in the weeks following did the band become the Jimi Hendrix Experience. The trio were together for just two years, recording most of the band's highly successful records before Jimi died in 1970.

*(photo credit: Ian Wright Northern Echo)*

**Autism and Musical Creativity**

"People with high autistic traits could be said to have less quantity but the greater quality of creative ideas." Martin Doherty, from UEA's School of Psychology.

"Music opens a window into the world of someone with autism. They might not be able to step into your world, so it's a privilege to use music to step into theirs." Steve, guitar teacher and BROCS Support Worker.

**Musicians and other artists with Autistic Spectrum Disorders**
From sources across the web:

Dan Aykroyd
Daryl Hannah
Anthony Hopkins
Elon Musk
Tim Burton
Bobby Fischer
Courtney Love
Eminem
Wolfgang Amadeus Mozart
David Byrne
Gary Numan
Woody Allen
Joe Walsh
Tara Palmer-Tomkinson
Steve Jobs
Stanley Kubrick
Lewis Carroll
James Joyce
Hans Christian Andersen

Statistically, it is likely that there are many more 'creatives' who have never been diagnosed.

## Eye-witness Report by David Billau

I was nineteen years old when I saw the Jimi Hendrix Experience in Darlington. And what an experience it was.

Whilst preparing to go out to our usual R&B club night at the Imperial Hotel, I was suddenly aware of Jimi's band being introduced on Top of the Pops. This was the then must-watch TV program for all young people, with four million tuning in every Thursday evening.

Pete Murray (I think?), saying 'And straight in at number seven in the chart, the Jimi Hendrix Experience with *Hey Joe.*' I watched and listened and thought he was pretty good on the guitar. I had never seen him play before that moment. Then, a dreadful thought occurred - if he was there on TV, he couldn't possibly be appearing in Darlington that night. Incredible though it may seem now, it didn't enter my head that I was watching a recording of a TV show filmed beforehand.

An old schoolmate, Brian Deighton who played bass with a local band, had seen him playing and insisted that he should not be missed. The Imperial was a fairly small venue, and apparently, there were about two hundred people there. These were mostly regulars to this 'club' and were familiar faces from schooldays and pubs etc around the town.

We were generally a 'regular' looking bunch of teenagers at the time. We had 'short back and sides' and were pretty 'clean-cut'. I don't think that the 'hippie cult' hit Darlo' until later in the sixties.

From memory, I don't believe there was even a proper stage, and we were all on the same floor level as the band. I got so close; I could have just reached out and touched Jimi! He was so exciting to look at!

Until that evening, my electric guitar inspiration had come from Hank Marvin of The Shadows. That all changed from the very first moment of hearing Jimi's guitar sound. I had never heard anything like it. The Troggs *Wild Thing* was the standout track for me. There was unbelievable volume and power.

So many years on now, I might reflect more on his appearance than just his music. Looking back, I realise how magnificent he looked. I had never seen anyone who looked anything like him. He had the presence and appearance of a tribal warrior, slightly menacing and unnerving, but I mean that in an entirely complimentary way. His individuality in his appearance as well as his music were awe-inspiring. It was life-changing for me in terms of music taste.

I wasn't aware that I could have probably gone downstairs to the Bolivar bar and seen, or even talked to him but instead made my way home with Jimi's guitar sound ringing in my ears. I knew nothing of the stolen guitar until I heard the story sometime later.

*~David Billau*

*Jimi wearing one of his military dress jackets complete with braid and gold buttons.
Photo by Ian Wright, Northern Echo.*

**Eye-witness Report by Maggie Gibson**

My friend Marilyn Rek arrived early and got a place at the front of the small stage. I couldn't believe Jimi Hendrix was performing at The Imperial R&B Club. The place was full of the usual clientele, all aged between seventeen and twenty-five. The same people went every week and there were few strangers even though Jimi was appearing. Everyone clambered to the front of the stage, so there was no room to dance.

The atmosphere was amazing. Compared to the usual blues bands, Jimi was off-the-scale. He was quite hypotonic to watch. I remember the time passed too quickly. The fashion then was for long leather/suede coats for both sexes, or rabbit skin coats for women. I will have been wearing my mum's green suede coat and my friend was wearing a gorgeous navy leather coat her mum had bought as a birthday present.

Everyone knew what to expect from him from his recent TV appearances, especially playing the guitar with his teeth, which had become his trademark. He didn't fail to deliver. I don't remember any on-stage banter from him other than announcing the names of the songs. However, he still managed to engage with the audience through his music. Everyone listened intently. There was not a lot of background talking, as often happened with lesser bands. I also remember the room went very dark when he came onto the stage and stayed like that while playing, apart from some dimmed lights on the stage.

I only found out about Jimi's missing guitar sometime after the event.
*~Maggie Gibson*

*Jimi Hendrix plays a right-handed white Stratocaster strung and held left-handed. Photo from Wikipedia*

## The Fender Stratocaster

The Fender Stratocaster, colloquially known as the Strat, is a model of electric guitar designed between 1952 and 1954 by Leo Fender, Bill Carson, George Fullerton, and Freddie Tavares.

The Fender Musical Instruments Corporation has continuously manufactured the Stratocaster since 1954. It is a double-cutaway guitar, with an extended top "horn" shape for balance. Along with the Gibson Les Paul, Gibson SG, and Fender Telecaster, it is one of the most emulated electric guitar shapes. "Stratocaster" and "Strat" are trademark terms belonging to Fender. Guitars that duplicate the Stratocaster by other manufacturers are sometimes called S-Type or ST-type guitars.

The "quacky" or "doinky" tone of the bridge and middle pickups in parallel, (was) popularized by players such as Jimi Hendrix, Stevie Ray Vaughan, David Gilmour, Rory Gallagher, Mark Knopfler, Bob Dylan, Eric Johnson, Nile Rodgers, George Harrison, Scott Thurston, Ronnie Wood, John Mayer, Ed King, Robert Cray.
Late 1960s Stratocaster with large "CBS" headstock, played left-handed (upside-down and reverse-strung) by Jimi Hendrix.

*(Source: Wikipedia, The Free Encyclopedia)*

```
Chris Lloyd, Chief Feature Writer at The
Northern Echo.
```

*Shergar has never been found, but everyone assumes Irish terrorists got hold of him. Lord Lucan is still missing but everyone presumes he is dead and a death certificate has been issued. Some mysteries are not really mysterious any more. But the story of Jimi Hendrix's guitar has no known conclusion. It just disappeared after a gig in the Imperial Quarter of this Quaker town – the Bermuda Triangle of Darlington. Fifty years later, there is still no resolution, although so many people have heard whispers, so many have theories and several have been sold fakes in the dark of High Row. Now James Vasey has cracked this compelling case and written the last chapter of this most marvellous of musical mysteries…*

## TABLE OF CONTENTS

Foreword by Bob Smeaton: ................................................................ 1
CHAPTER ONE ...................................................................... 3
CHAPTER TWO ...................................................................... 10
CHAPTER THREE .................................................................. 14
CHAPTER FOUR .................................................................... 23
CHAPTER FIVE ...................................................................... 29
CHAPTER SIX ........................................................................ 35
CHAPTER SEVEN .................................................................. 41
CHAPTER EIGHT ................................................................... 48
CHAPTER NINE ..................................................................... 54
CHAPTER TEN ....................................................................... 58
CHAPTER ELEVEN ................................................................ 64
CHAPTER TWELVE ................................................................ 69
CHAPTER THIRTEEN ............................................................. 75
CHAPTER FOURTEEN ............................................................ 84
CHAPTER FIFTEEN ................................................................ 90
CHAPTER SIXTEEN ............................................................... 93
CHAPTER SEVENTEEN .......................................................... 97
CHAPTER EIGHTEEN ............................................................. 105
CHAPTER NINETEEN ............................................................. 114
CHAPTER TWENTY ............................................................... 122
CHAPTER TWENTY ONE ....................................................... 134
CHAPTER TWENTY-TWO ...................................................... 141
CHAPTER TWENTY THREE ................................................... 144
CHAPTER TWENTY FOUR ..................................................... 148
CHAPTER TWENTY FIVE ...................................................... 155

## Foreword by Bob Smeaton:
## The Grammy-Award-Winning Director of 'Jimi Hendrix - Band of Gypsys'

*When a friend suggested I read this book I have to admit that I was slightly reluctant having read more books about Jimi Hendrix than any other musician or band I have previously made documentaries about. Ten pages in and I was hooked.*

*This was not yet another take on the Jimi Hendrix Story, in fact, it's a story based around a little-known event that occurred when the Jimi Hendrix Experience played a concert in Darlington in the North East of England back in 1967.*

*It was during or after this show that Jimi's black Stratocaster went 'missing'. The mystery surrounding this guitar has swirled around for four decades, and this book does not attempt to solve it. However, it is as good a guess as any as to what could have happened to it.*

*In setting the story in the 21st century, and mixing fact and fiction with Danny, a young autistic kid with a talent for playing the guitar as the main protagonist, I see parallels with how Richard Curtis introduced The Beatles to a younger generation through his film Yesterday.*

*Whether or not this book will achieve the level of success as that film is in the lap of the gods, but one thing is certain, 'that dude could play'.*

*~Bob Smeaton*

**CHAPTER ONE**

Where Jimi came from, they would describe the room as Bible-black. Just two spots and a single backlight illuminated the trio of musicians. Their long, unkempt hair cast strange shadows on the ceiling, while the brass buttons and military braid on the singer's jacket sent shards of light bouncing around like laser beams. The show had been billed as The Jimi Hendrix Experience, and it was way beyond the experience of Billy Curran and his mates from Darlington in the North of England.

Only the glowing trails of cigarette ends held in waving hands identified a few individuals amongst the tightly packed knot of two hundred swaying bodies. The air smelled of tobacco smoke, spilt beer, sweat, and an over-generous application of perfume and aftershave. The deep thump of drumbeats and bass guitar resonated in Billy's chest while the squealing guitar feedback from the amplifiers had the same effect on his ears. All this combined to overload the naive teenager's already confused senses. He needed to vomit. And to do it now.

James Vasey

On Thursday, February 2nd, 1967, Jimi Hendrix was booked to play at a weekly RnB club in Darlington, just a few months after he had arrived in England from the USA. His debut record, *Hey Joe,* had begun climbing the UK charts but was not yet a big hit. The artist behind the unique sound was still relatively unknown, other than to avid readers of the London-based, rock music press. The Animals' bassist, Chas Chandler, had brought the artist to England in search of the chart success that had eluded Jimi in America. Until he met Chas, Jimi had not written his own songs, which his mentor encouraged him to start doing. Chas was from Newcastle and used his fame and local connections to book a few appearances on the Northern club scene for the extraordinarily talented newcomer.

Billy Curran was with his two mates at the Darlington gig that night. Well, he called them mates, though in truth, by anyone else's standards, they were not real friends. But Billy had no others to compare them with. He was a bit slow, as people said back then, about anyone whose diffident behaviour could not otherwise easily be explained. His shyness and lack of social skills made him an easy target for mindless teenagers, two of whom had brought him along that night. Lacking any confidence themselves, they thought the awkward Billy made them look smarter and cooler. It was all relative.

Unused to alcohol in any form, Billy had consumed four pints of beer, but one of these had also been spiked with cheap vodka by his companions "for a laugh", they later confessed.

The small hotel ballroom booked for the performance was packed beyond its official capacity. There was no raised stage area to separate the band and audience. Instead, the trio performed on an old red, patterned carpet they had brought along for that purpose. Two sturdy roadies stood on either side of this rug, staring menacingly at anyone getting too close to an invisible line in front of the microphone stands.

Billy felt the bile rising in his throat and he sought a way out before the vomit could erupt over the rows of people in front of him. Behind him, he saw no way back through the solid mass of bodies. Ahead, past the make-do stage, he made out a red glow from a Fire

Escape sign. It was just visible through a gap in the velvet curtains that formed the backdrop to the band.

Without thinking, Billy lunged forward, pushing past swaying heads of long hair that could have belonged to girls or boys. Rushing forward with his head down, he stumbled past Jimi, knocking over the bassist's microphone stand, but somehow making it through the gap in the thick velvet curtains. Continuing his run backstage, he tripped over a tangled web of cables and fell headfirst against a fire door. The latch bar opened under his weight, precisely as it was designed to do, and Billy sprawled out into a dark, wet side street.

On his knees on the rain-soaked pavement, he vomited into the gutter. Behind him, the fire door sprang back, and the wind slammed it shut again, subduing the band's noise from a roar to a rumble.

After three or four minutes, the teenager had emptied the entire contents of his stomach into the gutter, and Billy struggled to his feet using a parked van as support. Then he saw the black and chrome electric guitar lying on the pavement next to him. Unknown to

Billy, the shiny black instrument had been leant against the inside of the fire door. Jimi had changed to his white Stratocaster mid-show, as he was prone to do if one got out of tune. Still drunk, Billy was drawn to the instrument like a magpie. Something compelled him to pick it up and run.

Billy's strict Catholic upbringing and ever-watchful parents, had, until that night successfully kept him away from trouble of any kind.

He woke the following morning feeling very hungover and extremely remorseful. He had run the short distance home in no time and, as far as he knew, unnoticed. He had almost pushed it out of his mind until he opened his eyes and saw it leaning against his bedroom wall accusingly, the ultimate reminder of what he had done. One broken string revealed the reason why Jimi hadn't been playing it at the moment Billy had stumbled through the fire door.

Hungover and unsure what to do with the guitar, he placed it in a large plastic bird feed bag, shaking dust and debris from inside before he did, then hid it in a hollow section of a wall of the pigeon loft in their small allotment garden. He wanted to erase the memory of that night, but the guilt he felt about that guitar haunted him for years. He didn't tell a single soul what he had done, and no one he knew ever mentioned the incident.

Although Danny did not see it, a review of the concert appeared in the *Northern Echo* the following day. The report also recorded the loss and assumed theft of Jimi's black Stratocaster guitar, valued at over one hundred pounds. This was a considerable sum in 1967 – an average month's wages and double what the band were paid to play the gig that night. Nevertheless, the loss of the guitar was not reported to the police. Jimi's band and manager had been invited to a party that night in Newcastle, along with the UK band Moody Blues and were keen to get there.

It was assumed by everyone that the guitar had been sold quickly and anonymously to a criminal receiver of stolen goods or a second-hand shop for the price of a few rounds of drinks. A stolen, off-the-shelf Stratocaster, belonging to a then largely unheard-of musician, was of no exceptional value and could have ended up anywhere. Those involved agreed that the likelihood was it would never reappear again, and even if it did, there would be no possible way to attribute it to Jimi.

**CHAPTER TWO**

The Pan Am flight that brought Jimi Hendrix to England touched down in the autumn of 1966. He was a totally unknown solo artist with no band, money or friends in the UK other than Chas Chandler, who had paid for his ticket. He arrived in London, strapped on his Stratocaster, and let that make his introductions. Jimi immediately caused a sensation in the swinging capital and everyone in the burgeoning pop music business wanted to see him play.

Between October 1966 and his arrival in Darlington on the 2$^{nd}$ of February 1967, he had caused every lead guitar player in Britain to re-think what they were doing. He chewed up the pop rule book and spat it out. The top musicians of the time, Keith Richards, Mick Jagger, Brian Jones, Jeff Beck, Paul McCartney, The Who, Eric Burdon, and John Mayall all turned up to see the American who Chas had brought to light a fire under British pop music. So impressed was Ringo Star that he loaned Jimi a flat in central London.

In those days, not every home had a television set on which to witness Jimi's UK TV debut in black and white on the pop series Ready Steady Go in December 1966. But those that did quickly spread the word. When Jimi turned up at the Imperial Hotel in Darlington a handful of weeks later, it was a sellout concert.

An odd assortment of local teenagers, many still undecided about which music tribe they belonged to, came to see what all the fuss was about. Mainstream pop fans mingled with blues fans and Soul Boys. The mixed audience suited Jimi because his musical style was by now very much his own. It was difficult to place in any convenient pigeonhole. He forced audiences to abandon all preconceptions and see this as the beginning of something new.

This freestyle music was undoubtedly the end of much that was predictable about the pop music business. The days of musicians dressing in suits and ties, which were only slightly modified versions of what their fathers and grandfathers wore, were drawing to a close. The conventions and structure of pop songs were being ripped up and thrown out, along with the regular four-piece band line-up. It appeared there was no rule too sacrosanct for Jimi to ignore.

Jimi opened the way and inspired English bands to throw off the conventions that had become the norms of popular music. Following him came a flood of an entirely new type of rock and pop music. This phenomenon rippled outward from London all around the world. For a tiny country, Britain was disproportionately well represented at the legendary Woodstock Festival in the United States just two years later. British bands would continue to dominate pop charts around the globe for many years to come. Some might argue that it all started with a black American who shook up London and inspired its musicians to be more creative.

Growing up poor in the still partly segregated United States, Jimi had endured enough rules as to where he could go, wait for a bus, relieve himself or sleep. He had served his apprenticeship playing guitar for soul, and rhythm and blues bands in the States. He even backed Little Richard when his band appeared on an American television show in 1965—dressed in the standard but incongruous uniform of black performers at that time - a hired dinner suit. This brief taste of life in the spotlight must have felt like a ticket to freedom to the young Jimi.

**CHAPTER THREE**

Billy was nearly forty years old and still living at home when he finally married. Average height, medium build, quietly spoken and soberly dressed, he was unremarkable in almost every way. Billy was easy to ignore and that was how he liked it. He preferred to stay under the radar where his insecurities were less likely to be noticed.

Jing was the widowed daughter of a family who ran his local Chinese takeaway. Outwardly she was almost as invisible as Billy except for kind eyes, usually hidden under a fringe, and a smile that transformed her face, on the few occasions that she used it. Billy had seen both features and was captivated.

It was a small business in a quiet neighbourhood on Billy's way home from work. Jing was the only woman Billy had any regular contact with, and certainly the only one he felt confident speaking to. She smiled patiently, listening to Billy complain about his boring job and his restrictive life with his parents. Meanwhile, her family cooked the takeaway food, which was his favourite Friday night treat when his parents went off to their caravan. Through these regular meetings, their unusual courtship was carried out.

Their marriage was as pragmatic as it was sudden. They both desperately wanted to get out of their respective family's control. Jing also needed emotional support and a father figure for her young daughter, Li.

Jing had been widowed when her husband died from tuberculosis less than a year after the birth of their child, having unwittingly brought the disease with him from Hong Kong. Billy had learned to manage his early awkwardness and had developed better social skills. The only remaining symptom of his childhood condition was a resistance to change and an almost obsessive tidiness. All his shirts were the same colour, he only wore one brand of jeans, and always ordered the same Chinese meal. Balancing this, Billy was kind and gentle and had held down a steady but low-paid job with the local council since leaving school.

Within a year, the newlyweds had a son, whom they called Danny. By the time the child was three, they knew something was amiss with his development. It took a further three years for a diagnosis of Danny being on the autistic spectrum. It was a couple more before they learned that he was at the lower end of symptom severity. This diagnosis meant that life would be a little easier for both Danny and his parents. Nevertheless, they were all going to face additional challenges.

Danny was a loving and affectionate child, but as he grew older, he remained distant and introverted compared to his peers. He preferred to inhabit a world of his imagination. He drew skilfully but often the same subject repeatedly with only slight variation. Highly numerate and with an astonishing memory, the child was clearly intelligent, but a short attention span impaired his ability to develop skills.

He learned quickly but wanted to move on to the next thing immediately. As a result, few things retained Danny's interest for long, and additional stimulus had to come from his imagination. Billy began to recognise in his son some of the issues he had struggled with himself, but without the benefit of a diagnosis. Autism had been a little understood condition when Billy was growing up.

## Hope the Dude Can Play

One day, when Danny was in his teens, Li brought an acoustic guitar home on loan from school. The boy seemed captivated by the sound the strings made, despite Li only having learned three chords and seldom able to play any of those correctly. Danny picked up the guitar when Li got bored with her practice session. He placed his fingers in the same frets as Li had and strummed the three chords she tried to play, but this time they sounded good. The family looked on in astonishment as he repeated the exercise his stepsister had been struggling with for over thirty minutes. While she had referred to a book with finger instructions, Danny had committed the fret positions to memory and played the notes instinctively. His parents applauded enthusiastically.

"That's just not fair," Li complained bitterly. "I get it that he needs more support, which we give him, but then he goes and pulls off stunts like that. Sometimes I hate him."

This was a rare outburst for teenager Li. She had taken a back seat for most of her life while more attention had been lavished on Danny's greater needs.

She had always shown remarkable patience and maturity despite the compromises that had often meant.

Billy took Li's hand and took her to one side. "I know it's tough sometimes. You are a brilliant sister and a wonderful daughter. And remember, you can do so many things that Danny can't and probably never will. He's extremely good at just a few things. Let him enjoy those moments."

Billy kissed Li on the top of her head, and she forced a smile back at him.

Despite its unpromising beginnings, with neither set of parents approving of the match, Jing and Billy's marriage had worked, and Danny's birth was the turning point. The challenges that could easily have driven them apart drew them closer together. From the start, Billy worked very hard to be a first-rate father, but in the end, he found it came naturally. Li faced some challenges at school because of her ethnicity, and Danny even more so because of his condition, but these external threats became the glue that bound them together as a family. In times of difficulty, Billy would hug them in a huddle and repeat his mantra, "It's us against the world."

Each time Li returned home from school with new chords and combinations to learn, Danny mastered them in a fraction of the time that she could, and remembered them all the following day while his sibling could not. None of them had ever seen Danny so engaged in a single activity for so long. He was happy to practice until his fingers hurt and he had no choice but to stop.

He learned that by moving his finger positions and changing the pressure, there was an almost limitless variation to the sound that could be created. This challenge was that it was virtually impossible to master the instrument entirely or to run out of ways to be creative. It became an all-consuming passion for Danny, but soon term ended for the summer, and the school's guitar had to be returned.

Both parents had low-income jobs. With two children at school, including one with additional needs, the family had little spare money for luxuries such as guitars. But then Billy remembered his teenage secret still hidden in the pigeon loft at his parents' house.

After nearly forty years, the old guitar was filthy when he retrieved it from its hiding place. What had been a shiny black body was now dull and tarnished. The chrome fittings had traces of rust, and the body had fragments of bird feed that had clung to the inside of the bag. In addition, it still had one snapped string, a detail he had completely forgotten about. He cleaned the Stratocaster with car polish and purchased some cheap replacement strings. When he had finished, he decided it looked as good as when he had first seen it glinting in the streetlights on that rainy night in 1967.

When Billy handed him the surprise, Danny seemed underwhelmed. This was the reaction they had come to expect from someone who found it hard to mask his emotions to avoid hurting the feelings of others. The Stratocaster differed greatly from the acoustic guitar's shape, weight, and wood finish. Danny was also resistant to change or deviance from what he considered the norm.

However, when he noticed that the strings on the Strat were fitted upside down compared to those on the acoustic, he recognised something he could put right. Jimi had famously been a left-handed player of right-handed guitars. It took Danny only five minutes to re-string it, following the pattern in his head from the school's instrument.

He strummed the shiny black guitar to check the tuning and was both surprised and disappointed by the dull, lifeless sound. There was hardly any volume compared to the acoustic guitar. Billy explained that an electric guitar needed an amplifier to make it sound as it should. Then it would not only sound better but also much louder.

He promised that if Danny learned to play all the chords in his stepsister's books and the half dozen songs at the back of it, he would buy him an amplifier, "But it might have to be a second-hand one," he added. This task should have taken a student of his age three months of practice; instead, in less than two weeks, Danny had completed it all. His father had to obtain a credit agreement to buy the cheapest amplifier in the music shop. Trying the newly electrified guitar for the first time was a pivotal moment. Danny's life would never be the same from that day forward. For Billy, it was the re-opening of the wound he thought had been healed by time. The guilt he felt over keeping the guitar had never entirely left him, even though he had kept it buried for a very long time. Deciding whether to exhume it from its hiding place had created a huge dilemma for Billy. He knew how much difference the instrument could make to Danny's life, but he could not help being concerned about its potential to bring trouble to his own.

**CHAPTER FOUR**

A year later, Danny's progress in playing guitar had been dramatic, but it had become clear to Billy that he needed a professional teacher to continue improving. However, paying for private lessons seemed out of the family's reach. Billy only knew one person who might be able to help, but he had not spoken to him in nearly forty years and had no idea how he might make contact. He went to the Cricket Club, where his friends had met and socialised as young men. It had been one of the few places in Darlington to serve alcohol to teenagers without asking too many questions about their age.

Little about the pace had changed. It might have had a lick of paint since the last time he had been there, but he was pretty sure that it was the same carpet. He suspected that if he looked hard enough, he would be able to find the odd cigarette burn from the days before the introduction of the smoking ban. Even if it wasn't the same carpet that had been there forty years before, it had certainly been there for some time.

"Bloody Hell. Look who it is!" was the greeting Billy received just seconds after he walked through the doors.

"Is that really you, Billy?"

Stick was no longer quite as slim as when he had earned his nickname, but it had stayed with him. His nose was bright red, while the rest of his face was deathly pale. He did not look like a picture of health, Billy thought. He seemed so comfortable on the bar stool next to the jukebox, as if he'd been there since Billy had last seen him. That was not far short of the truth.

"You come to buy me a pint?"

"No, I've come to collect the one you owe me for spiking my drink at that Jimi Hendrix gig."

"Eeeeh. What a night that was. We saw Jimi play live. There's not many can say that."

"Aye, but plenty in Darlington claim to have been there, but they never were," Billy quipped.

"True. The Imperial would have had to have the capacity of The Albert Hall to accommodate all the folk who say they saw him that night. I know at least three people who reckon they know where Jimi's missing Strat is right now," Stick added.

Billy's legs nearly gave way when he heard this, and he felt that his face would surely give away his guilty secret.

"But I know they are all full of shit. One guitar authenticated to have been played by Jimi recently sold in the USA for a million dollars. The Strat from his earliest UK concerts and recordings could be worth a million quid today. There's no way some skint loser in Darlington has been sitting on that kind of cheque without trying to cash it."

"Is that so?" Billy said, smiling, relieved that the many stories about the missing guitar were no closer to the truth.

"Aye, but my theory is that it's still out there somewhere. It's probably under several coats of new paint and being played by someone in a fifty-quid-a-night R&B band. They'll have no idea what they have in their hands and no way of ever finding out. That's the only logical explanation for why it has never surfaced since the day it was taken. The person who nicked it will have cashed it in the following day for a tenner. Let's face it: none of us knew then that Jimi would become a global superstar. He was just an odd-looking yank who could get weird noises from a guitar."

At this point, the club steward appeared to take Billy's order.

"He's been getting free beer off that Jimi Hendrix story for as long as I have been here. We've had strangers turning up to meet the man who shook hands with Jimi Hendrix."

"Well, not this time," Billy said, laughing, "because I was there that night and I know he was so pissed he fell asleep during the support act before Jimi even played a note. He's paying for my beer, and I'll have a pint of Strongarm, please."

The steward laughed out loud, but Stick did not appear to enjoy the joke at his expense.

The pair settled onto their stools and Stick changed the subject to ask what Billy had been up to for the last four decades.

"So, you are looking for a guitar teacher for your kid. Top-notch but really cheap. That might be a tough call. However, you might just be in luck."

Stick drained the last dregs from his glass, leaving only the foam from the head. He placed his empty glass on the bar and stared silently at Billy.

"Ah, OK. Give him another pint, steward."

"Cordless Chris. That's yer man."

Stick explained that he used to be known as Chris the Lick, who played with various bands for over twenty years and enjoyed some success. He had appeared on Top Of The Pops twice, Later with Jools Holland, and had writing credits on several recordings.

"So, why the name change?"

"Chris was helping unload the band's gear from a van outside a venue when a clumsy roadie dropped a Marshall stack amplifier on his left hand. It crushed his fingers against the steel edge of the truck bed. The surgeons saved them, but he lost any practical control over the three central fingers. The band had no insurance. Overnight, Chris became unemployed, unemployable, and broke. He could use two of the fingers to give his former bandmates the V-sign but that was the extent of their usefulness."

"Hence Chord-less Chris?" Billy guessed.

"You've got it. With his left hand shattered but the right still working fine, Chris taught himself to play slide guitar pretty well. However, there's little call for Hawaiian style, or country and western bands, in Middlesbrough, so he can't make any money from that. I heard he had tried offering lessons, but a single-handed guitar player sounds about as credible as a one-legged football coach."

"So, he knows his stuff but will also be cheap," Billy said.

"Desperate for money, I would imagine," Stick confirmed.

**CHAPTER FIVE**

When Chris arrived at Billy's house a week later, he had no guitar, just a battered laptop. Billy had warned him that Danny did not like meeting strangers and probably would not speak to him at first. The injured guitar player did not try to make small talk. He plugged in his laptop and connected it to the amplifier he had brought along.

A YouTube clip started to play showing a younger Chris on stage at what appeared to be a large auditorium packed with people. The clip caption was Live at The Festspielhaus Baden-Baden. The band were playing a medley of Jimi Hendrix songs and nailing them. Danny looked sideways at Chris and then back to the young man on the screen, double-checking that this was the same person. The audience was going wild – clapping, cheering, and singing along to the choruses.

Danny picked up his Strat and tried to imitate some of the hand positions he saw Chris using.

"That's really good, Danny. You've even got the perfect guitar. A classic Stratocaster just like one Jimi played."

Billy interjected with an unnecessary cover story, "My dad bought me that guitar from a pawn shop when I was twenty-one, but I never learned to play; Danny's taken to it like a duck to water. He's taught himself by just listening."

"So did Jimi." Chris pointed out. "His family couldn't afford lessons."

Chris used his good right hand to adjust Danny's finger positions on the neck.

"Jimi's fingers were longer than yours, so you need to arch your hand more to get the same pressure he would."

The teenager didn't say anything but did as he was told. When he played the few notes again, he smiled, realising it did sound better that way. So the seeds of an odd relationship were sown, but it was not without its difficulties. There were tantrums when Danny could not duplicate finger position and hand movements as he was shown. But Chris was a remarkably patient teacher. One day, about a month into their sessions, the older man suddenly became furious at Danny's constant impatience at not getting it right at the first attempt.

Chris was having a few problems of his own, facing a lot of financial pressure at home. Money was always tight, and his wife had been questioning the logic of him giving lessons at such low rates and wasting expensive fuel to travel to deliver them. He would have done it for nothing if he could, partly to get out of the house and away from the nagging. He also saw a talent in this challenging kid and enjoyed nurturing it. But he did expect his efforts to be appreciated, and Danny did not always oblige. Sometimes, to Chris, he seemed downright rude.

One day Chris's frustration boiled over. Holding his limp digits in front of Danny's face, he blazed at him, "Anyone would think it was you who was handicapped. Well, you're mistaken; it's my hand that doesn't work. That's a real fucking handicap." He continued to rant. "Not only are these useless, but they ache in the winter and swell up in the summer. I'd be better off without them; At least I'd get a disability allowance to stop the wife nagging me. Instead, I get a rude, ungrateful teenager who thinks he knows everything."

His tirade continued spilling out years of pent-up anger and frustration. "You! You want everything to be perfect instantly! Well, life doesn't work like that, Danny. Even after playing Woodstock and being acclaimed by all his contemporaries, Jimi still practised every day, trying to get better. He wanted to learn more and perfect ways of getting different sounds from his Strat."

Chris's anger subsided and his tone softened, "Next time you feel sorry for yourself, think of me. I'll never play All Along The Watch Tower ever again. My fingers will no longer reach those hard-to-get notes like Jimi did. You have as much talent as me - maybe even more. You need to listen and practice more. You could eventually play Hendrix better than me and I want to be the first to witness that. Could you do that for me? Let me play through your fingers. Allow me to feel the power of that black Strat. If not for me, then do it for Jimi's memory."

No one had ever spoken to Danny like this before, like a grown-up and an equal, 'let alone swear at him. He saw the passion burning in Chris's hazel green eyes and the tears welling in their corners. Danny's family had tip-toed around his frustrated mood swings all his life. Even his teachers had given him more latitude than he was probably entitled to. Now, he wanted to play at least as good as, or even better than Chris. Not just for himself, but for his teacher and mentor. He wanted this more than he had ever wanted anything in his life.

Danny was fast becoming an accomplished virtuoso guitar player, while Li, encouraged by her stepfather and Chris, agreed to learn to play the bass guitar. She spent hour after hour watching tutorials on YouTube even though she had yet to get hold of an instrument. She was not sure how she was going to get hold of one, but she was going to do it somehow.

Billy had returned to his parents to retrieve his old vinyl albums. Without any encouragement from his father, Danny's favourites were the Jimi Hendrix songs with their fluid guitar solos.

Li also introduced Danny to Tom, a drummer from school, with a thin, straggly beard that he thought made him look older but didn't. A computer game addict, Tom's only physical exercise and emotional release came from beating the drum skins with sticks. And he was good at it.

Without ever planning it, they had become a band.

**CHAPTER SIX**

The early rehearsals were not easy.

Tom was the only one of the three of them who had played with other musicians before. He was quick to pick up on what was needed in a song and find the groove. He had a good repertoire of skills and could replicate a pattern of beats he heard on a performance pretty quickly. The only reasons why he might not sound exactly like a recording were largely down to the limitations of his kit, but the truth was that he was more than capable of driving the band at the level they were likely to be able to play at. Most importantly of all, he could hold the beat like a metronome, and if that was all that was needed as the other pair learned their parts, he was happy to do that.

Danny played by instinct, his fingers finding the notes unerringly, but he needed to develop his technique and that was clear in the frustration that occasionally showed itself. He wanted to be able to play all kinds of things that were beyond his abilities, but that didn't stop him from trying. No matter how much he watched footage of Hendrix playing, there was still the need to fill in the gaps when the camera panned away from what his hands were doing. Thankfully, the lessons he was getting from Chris were making a real difference.

Li was finding it all more of a challenge.

She had found it hard enough trying to learn to play the acoustic guitar, and Danny had soon outstripped her on that. Now he had the Stratocaster, he was no longer interested in the instrument that Li had found hard to master even the basics of. And yet somehow it had been decided that she should play an instrument she had never picked up before. It had somehow been assumed that she would take up the role without a single thought as to how she would raise the money to buy one, and the amplifier to go with it.

She should have said no. She should have suggested that they ask someone like Jason Smith-Booth who was in the last year of school, just like her. He could already play guitar and was looking to start his own band. What's more, his dad was loaded, so getting hold of the equipment would be a lot easier for him than it would be for her.

## Hope the Dude Can Play

She should definitely have said no, but she hadn't. Instead, she had lain awake at night, trying to work out how she would raise the cash.

She was already working at weekends in her grandparents' takeaway and had managed to save some money, but it was nowhere near enough to even buy something second-hand. She had headed into town the first chance she'd had, only to have her suspicions confirmed. Even if she spent every penny of the money she had saved, she was still a long way short of what she would need. She was still feeling down when she arrived at her grandparents' place to start work.

Her grandfather had seen straight away that something was bothering her, and he kept pushing her until she let it all spill out.

"I'll buy it for you," he said. "Let's call it an early birthday present.

She shook her head. "I can't let you do that, Grandfather. If I'm going to do this, I have to do it myself or not at all."

"Then call it a loan," he said. "You can pay me back out of your wages."

Her face suddenly lit up. "Would you really do that?"

"Of course," he said. "How does five pounds a week sound?"

It didn't take long for them to agree terms, after which he announced that he was giving her a pay rise anyway which covered most of the repayment. What's more, he seemed just as excited as she was and insisted that they had time to pick the equipment up before the shop closed for the rest of the weekend. And from the moment they placed the bass guitar and the amplifier into the boot of her grandfather's car, all she could think about was getting it back home.

She had tried it in the shop, surprised by the weight when she adjusted the strap, feeling the buzz when it was plugged into the amp. She hadn't wanted to say that she'd never played a bass before, but she had already watched countless tutorials on the internet, her fingers moving in time with the instructors, and with deliberation, she repeated one of the exercises. It felt good. It felt right, and she couldn't keep the smile from her face.

"Nice action," the salesman said. "That'll serve you well." Then he seemed to remember something and asked them to wait for a moment. He returned a few minutes later carrying a battered case that looked like it needed a clean.

"This has been in the back of the storeroom for years, and there's no way we're going to sell it. It came in when someone traded in a few pieces of gear. It's yours if you want it."

"I…" she started to say, knowing that she could not afford a penny more, and wasn't about to ask her grandfather for another penny.

The man waved his free hand. "I don't want anything for it. In fact, you'll be giving me a little extra space and save me making a trip to the local tip."

"Thank you," she said, her smile beaming even brighter.

"It's fine," he said. "When you've made your first million, come and buy a new one."

Li and her grandfather were still laughing about it when they reached the takeaway, though he had to admit that he had no idea why she would want to play something like that.

A few days later, the three of them got together for their first practice.

**CHAPTER SEVEN**

Danny had been annoyed about something. For days he had been practising one song, following a video he'd found on YouTube of a live performance, determined to be note-perfect. He had decided that they should start with *Hey Joe* and neither of the others had disagreed. The truth was that they knew if they tried to get him to start with a different song it would only lead to endless disagreements without anything changing. When Danny got something in his head, it was hard to change his mind.

It didn't matter to Li which song they learned first. She had to start somewhere, and this was as good as anywhere. She had managed to get hold of the notation for the bass part as it was recorded, but she was having trouble mastering it, and her fingers were sore by the time she put her instrument down. She had hated the idea of anyone listening as she made her first stumbling steps, and had plugged a pair of headphones into the amp. It helped her to hear what she was playing while drowning out the noise that Danny was making somewhere else in the house.

When Tom arrived for their first get-together, Danny was annoyed that he hadn't brought all his kit with him, even though he had arrived fully laden.

"Then you should have offered to give me a hand to carry it here," Tom said, a little tetchily "We can all go and get the rest of it if you like. But you'll have to help me carry it back when we've finished." Luckily, he only lived a couple of streets away.

Danny was about to complain that he was already set up to start, and it wasn't his fault that Tom hadn't thought ahead, but then he caught a look from his sister. He knew that look well; it was a reminder that he was in danger of saying something without thinking, and he stopped himself. With a heavy sigh that could have been heard in the next room, he unplugged his guitar and set it down, switching his amplifier off.

"Let's get on with this," he said. "We've wasted enough time already."

It took them almost an hour to walk to Toms's house and back again, and for Tom to set up his kit. They had to push the furniture in the cramped front room back to the wall to create enough space, but eventually, they were all ready.

"Hope you've both learned your parts," Danny said, but didn't wait for their reply. Instead, he simply launched himself into the opening, leaving the others in his wake.

It was chaos.

Li struggled to keep pace while Tom had trouble in finding and maintaining the beat. Eventually, he crashed his cymbals then threw his sticks down.

"What the hell are you playing at?" Danny demanded.

"What am *I* playing at?" Tom asked. "You're not listening to the rest of us, you're just pushing on when there's obviously a problem.

"I don't have a problem," Danny said. "I learned my part, but it sounds like you two haven't bothered."

Then suddenly everyone was talking at once, voices getting louder as each of them tried to make themselves heard. None of them noticed at first when the door opened, and Danny's mother appeared in the doorway.

"Keep the shouting down, please. The neighbours will think that your father is trying to kill me and call the police." It was enough to silence the three of them who gave their mumbled apologies before she left them to it.

"That doesn't change anything," Danny said, though he kept his voice as little more than a whisper.

"You're right, it doesn't," Tom said. "But if we're a band, we need to listen to each other. And I don't just mean what we're saying, but what we're playing."

"Well if you both listened to me…" Danny started, but Tom cut him off.

"I'm sorry Danny, but it's not just about you."

"But this is my band…"

"That's as may be, but if you don't listen, you won't have a band."

"Then let's just try it again."

"Not without us working out what went wrong," Tom said.

"Okay, well as you're the one who has all the answers, let's hear what you have to say."

"Alright," Tom said and retrieved his sticks. "The main problem is that we are not playing in time. You're playing all the notes in the right order but not always at the right speed."

"But I'm doing it exactly like Jimi did."

"That's as maybe, but if you've been learning by watching a video of him, there's every chance that we've been learning by watching something different, by just listening to the record, or maybe learning from a chart. If you want us to copy one particular performance exactly, we all need to be taking our cues from the same one."

Danny pursed his lips and nodded, but there was no outburst this time.

"The other thing is that Li is struggling to keep up," Tom said and turned to her. "You're trying really hard, but we need to simplify what you're playing, to start with at least."

She nodded and gave a smile, but it was Danny who burst in. "But it won't be the same then…"

"Maybe not, but we're all just learning to play together. If we can make a decent fist of this, we can improve as we go along."

"Okay smart arse, you seem to know everything. What do you suggest?"

"Well let's start by keeping it simple. *Hey Joe* has four beats to the bar." He started to tap out a steady beat using only his bass drum, his right foot operating the pedal that created the *thump, thump, thump, thump*. "See if you can keep pace with it, Li. If you can't, then miss a note rather than play it too slowly. If you just end up playing on every other beat that's fine."

Li joined in tentatively at first but then her pattern of playing fell into line with Tom's drum. Now that she had something to guide her, the hard work she'd been putting in started to pay off. She missed a few notes, but that didn't matter.

"I think we've got this," Tom said. "Join in whenever you're ready."

Now it was Danny's turn to look uncertain. He placed his fingers on the string to form the opening chord, but he resisted playing it. Eventually, he joined in and realised that Tom had been right, he needed to listen to what the others were doing. And as he lost himself in his playing, he was only barely aware that Tom was adding more embellishments.

Danny couldn't be sure what they sounded like, but they *felt* like a band, and they all had smiles on their faces.

**CHAPTER EIGHT**

The quality of Danny's guitar playing encouraged the other two to practice harder until they became a polished three-piece band. When Danny heard Li's idea to play on stage in front of a live audience of their peers, he locked himself in his room. He would only come out once his father came home. Danny relented when Billy promised he would not be forced to perform outside their house.

Rather than give up, Li, who knew her stepbrother well, applied some homegrown psychological strategy. First, she asked one of her friends, who Li could tell Danny was keen on, to call at their house during one of their rehearsals.

Kat was something of an oddball amongst her contemporaries. A free spirit. Her mum was both mother and father to her, her dad having died when she was young, but that had bound them close together. It had kept her mother young, but it sometimes made Kat seem older than her years. She had a very prominent metal brace on her teeth, dyed her hair pink, and wore an offbeat assortment of fashion styles with little makeup. Li saw she was naturally pretty in an understated way. Kat was also smart, kind and really into her music. She was seldom seen without earpieces, immersed in the music of some new band.

After hearing Danny play, Kat told him he was incredibly talented and asked if she could come to hear more and bring a friend. In this way, the audience that began as just Kat, grew by stealth. One extra school friend attended each rehearsal until their front room could hold no more. They all saw the awkward child transform into a more confident young person once he had a guitar strap around his neck and now a girl by his side.

Eventually, Danny and Li's parents' patience began to grow a little thin, or at least their neighbours did. They wanted to encourage them both in their music, but there had been complaints about the noise. It had been inevitable really, and in a way, they were lucky to have been able to carry on for as long as they did.

More and more friends wanted to come along and listen to them, and the front room was just too small to accommodate them all. They needed to find somewhere else to practice, and help came from an unexpected source.

The music teacher had heard about Danny's band, and after checking with the headmaster, had offered them the use of his room for a couple of hours after school. It seemed like the perfect solution. The caretaker was perfectly happy with the arrangement as he would be on the premises anyway as there were some adult education classes taking place until eight thirty in other parts of the building.

Tom's dad had kindly helped ferry all of their gear to the school in his car though he had drawn the line at carrying it all up to the second floor where the music room was. It took them two trips, but it was worth it. They felt they finally had a space where they could practice without worrying about annoying anyone.

On the second day of practice though, they had an unexpected visitor; Jason Smith-Booth, and he was carrying an expensive-looking guitar case. Everyone was surprised to see him, including the handful of girls who had come along to listen, just as they had before.

"I heard you were putting a band together," he said. "I thought you might need another guitar player."

"You heard wrong," Danny said. "We already are a band."

"Fair enough," Jason said. "But that doesn't mean you couldn't make it better." He glanced at the amplifiers that Danny and Li were using.

"I've got microphones and stuff too, if you haven't got any."

The others watched open-mouthed as he plugged in his amp and then took his guitar from its case; it looked shiny and new, unlike the old and worn instruments that Danny and Li were using. Clearly, he hadn't taken the hint.

"It's a Gibson," he said. "My dad bought it for me for my birthday."

He formed a chord and ran a plectrum across the strings. It might only have been a small amp he was using but it still produced a fair amount of power. "So what are we playing?" he asked, as if he hadn't heard Danny telling him that he was surplus to requirements.

"Wild Thing," Li said before Danny could tell him in no uncertain terms that he should leave.

"Great," he said. "I know that one."

But he didn't. Or at least he didn't know the Hendrix version and was soon standing there, helplessly trying to find his way into the song.

"You're playing it wrong," he said.

"No," Danny replied. "*You're* playing it wrong, and you can see that we don't need you. So if you could leave us to it, that would be great."

"But…"

"Look, we're fine as we are," Danny said. "We don't need you. We don't need your flash new guitar or the fancy equipment that your daddy can buy. And we certainly don't want someone who's not much of a guitar player, so get lost."

He was a lot more polite than he thought he was going to be, but he then turned his back on Jason to face the other two, to the sound of a couple of the girls giggling.

"Let's do that again, shall we?" Soon they were off again, oblivious to Jason packing his gear away. They only knew that he had left when the door slammed shut behind him.

**CHAPTER NINE**

Dannys's self-assurance grew as he witnessed the respect his guitar playing earned amongst his peers. He also enjoyed the attention it gained from the girls who had previously ignored him, and the boys who had teased or bullied him. His mother was shocked the first time she saw the band play. "My shrinking violet has bloomed into an orchid?" was all she said, her eyes full of tears of joy.

Although becoming, formally, girlfriend and boyfriend had never been specifically discussed, Kat felt that was their status. It was certainly what most people around them thought. So, she began to get a little jealous about the attention Danny was receiving, particularly from the other girls in her class. Even some of the older sixth formers were whispering his name flatteringly. She was also annoyed that Danny seemed to enjoy it. Without thinking it through, Kat decided to see if she could make Danny feel equally jealous.

"Jason Smith-Booth has asked me if I want to go to a concert with him. He says he has two tickets for Coldplay in Newcastle."

Without hesitating, Danny responded in the offhand manner to which he often defaulted when he was distracted. "Smith-Booth? Really? Go if you want. He's a crap guitar player and so are they." He turned away just before he could witness the devastation he had reaped on Kat's fragile feelings. The tearful teenager ran off before anyone saw her crying.

Although she was not very keen, Kat felt that she now had to go to the concert with Jason. Otherwise, she would lose even more respect. At first, he seemed very attentive and kind. Taller and heavier, he looked and sounded more mature than Danny. However, when there was a guitar solo in the band's performance, Jason could not resist saying, "That's better than that simpleton, Danny, don't you think?"

"Simpleton? What exactly do you mean by that?"

"Well, he's not all there upstairs, is he?" Jason sneered. "I bet he's not a hundred per cent downstairs, either, eh?" he added, laughing and winking.

That was the last straw for Kat. She got up and, without explanation, left Jason where he sat and travelled home alone. As the train made its way south to Darlington, Kat pondered the nonsensical attraction she felt for Danny. Jason was more handsome, stronger, taller and in some way more mature, and yet she disliked him, now more than before. Danny was self-absorbed, skinny, and odd-looking. He had been neglectful to the point of appearing uncaring, yet she liked him. She liked him a lot.

Something about strapping on a guitar elevated the wearer, not just to an audience but also to the players themselves. She remembered from nursery school that if you provided children with a cupboard full of toys, boys would come out with a sword or a gun every time. Boys had always been drawn to weapons. So, was a guitar empowering like a weapon seemed to be?

Or was it perhaps something phallic? Kat smiled at this naughty thought but acknowledged she might be thinking along the right lines. She had seen Jason's thrash metal band play at school, and he made the guitar look like both a weapon and a dick extension, simultaneously threatening and gross. Yet when Danny played the same instrument, he handled the guitar like a grown-up would a woman, or at least that was her impression from movies she had seen.

Female guitar players Kat had seen appeared emancipated by wearing an electric guitar. And yet, she thought an acoustic version had a softer, more feminine effect.

**CHAPTER TEN**

One night, after Danny's band, still in search of a name, had played at a school sixth-form party, Tom said to Li, "Have you noticed what happens to your brother when he plays those Hendrix numbers?"

"Jimi is his favourite," was all she could think of saying.

The drummer shook his head. "It's more than that. For sure, he's a good player, but something special happens when he plays that guitar on those songs. His smile broadens and his eyes glaze over like he's in a trance. It is like some mystical power turbo-charges his whole performance."

"I think I know what you mean. It's sometimes like it's not Danny playing, as if someone else has taken over his body. Whatever it is, it works; people love it. I love it. Even if the ease with which he acquired his talent infuriates me sometimes. I've practised twice as hard and am still not half as good."

Li learned that an agency looking to recruit musicians for a Hendrix Experience live stage show was staging a battle-of-the-bands-type competition.

## Hope the Dude Can Play

The ad said that the ability to play was more important than appearance, as that could be addressed by makeup, wigs, and costumes. The judges were to include a well-known session guitar player, a successful talent agent, and Lucinda Buckingham, Jimi's longtime English girlfriend who had toured extensively with the band. So, without telling the others, Li sent off an application and some live recordings of their cover versions. The only problem was that the band still didn't have a name, and she needed one to complete the form. She stared at it for more than ten minutes before she could think of anything that Danny would not object to. But when the name popped into her head she was sure that he would love it. Spirit of Jimi.

That morning, Danny asked Li if she had spoken to Kat in the last few days. His stepsister pulled no punches in telling Danny what a fool he was for not seeing that he had upset her.

"You can't talk to girls like that. Or anyone, for that matter. You need to stop and think before you speak, Danny. Anyway, she's dumped you, and frankly, I don't blame her. She's too good for you."

Danny was shocked. He was just beginning to learn that saying the first thing that came into his head was not a good idea. He had not meant to hurt her feelings. He just had not thought about them. The prospect of not having Kat around filled Danny with dread. It took him a while to accept any new situation, but if he did and they became the norm, he hated anyone changing them again. He realised how much he liked Kat and had become used to her being part of his life. Now, he desperately wanted her back, but perhaps it was already too late.

After lessons were over, Li and Tom arrived at the rehearsal room before Danny. He had to attend a special one-to-one session to help with his autism. His guitar was not on its stand where it would normally be, and they assumed he must have been in earlier and taken the Strat away to practice. Li turned on her bass amplifier and tuned up while Tom practised a few beats. Later, when a sad-looking Danny walked in carrying a bag but no guitar, Li asked, "Haven't you forgotten something?"

Instinctively, Danny looked to his now empty guitar stand, and it was as if the blood drained from his face. He froze for a moment, swayed slightly and then toppled like a felled tree, hitting his head heavily against a desk. Blood instantly oozed from a wound above his eye as the others scrambled to get to him over a tangle of wires and guitar peddles. Danny was out cold. Tom rushed to get help while Li held her stepbrother's blood-soaked head, tears pouring down her face.

When his father arrived at the hospital, Danny was hooked up to a drip, still unconscious with a bandage around his head. Li was holding one of his pale hands and a tearful Kat held the other.

"What the hell happened?" Billy asked. "The school just said he fell and banged his head."

Nearly in tears, Li answered softly, "He fainted or had some kind of a seizure when he realised that his guitar had gone. On top of the stress of Kat dumping him, the thought of losing his precious Stratocaster was too much for him. He banged his head badly as he fell."

"Why is he still unconscious?" Billy asked.

"He is just sedated. He got really anxious when he first came around. He was flailing his arms about and shouting. The staff couldn't examine him properly to see if there was any further damage, so they gave him something to sedate him."

"But he's OK?"

"He's had a brain scan," Li said. "And they think he will be fine apart from a slight scar on his forehead."

"Thank God for that."

"But he won't be fine."

"Why, what do you mean?"

"His guitar has gone," she said. "You should have seen him earlier when he came around. There was no consoling him. He would rather have lost an eye than that guitar."

"I'll save up. I'll get another just like it," Billy promised.

Li then told Billy about the competition she had entered their band into, adding that she had just heard they had been accepted.

"It starts in three weeks in London. We'll need to get train tickets, or maybe hire a van if we can get someone to drive. And find somewhere to stay."

Billy changed places with Li to let her take a break.

When she had left the room, he mumbled under his breath, "Oh fuck! How can I pay for all this? And buy a new guitar."

Danny began to stir. When he opened his eyes, he discovered that Kat had heard the news and rushed to the hospital. He squeezed her hand tightly and half-smiled for the first time in over a week.

**CHAPTER ELEVEN**

Danny was allowed to leave the hospital with his parents the following evening. He had been given some mild tranquilisers to try to keep him calm, but the effect soon wore off.

"But why haven't you called the police, Dad," Danny shouted for the third time, each cry getting louder.

"Because we don't know for sure that it has been stolen. Someone might just have borrowed it," Billy said, not even believing his own words.

Jing joined in, "Anyway, the school said that the police were not interested in petty thefts on campus. The school said they would conduct their own checks on their CCTV."

"Petty thefts! That's crap!" Danny railed. "Of course it's been stolen. My guitar is worth more to me than anything. I want it back. Please call the police, Mum."

Billy looked panicky. "I have told you there's no point," he said harshly. "I will buy you another guitar as soon as I can afford it. That's the best I can do."

"I don't want a new guitar. I just want my old Stratocaster back."

Billy couldn't bear the pressure any longer; he stormed out of the house and went for a walk to cool down. His parting words were, "You are all forbidden from calling the police. Do you hear me?"

Later that evening, when the teenagers were in their rooms and Billy was alone with his wife, he began to sob like a child. Jing held him in her arms and said, "It will be OK. I will ask my parents for the money for a new guitar."

"Jing, your parents have never liked me. They have always favoured Li over Danny because she is all Chinese. They think Danny is the way he is because of me. And they are probably right."

"That's not fair, Billy. They always try to be even-handed, but they are very traditional people. Mixed marriage is something very strange to them. They do their best."

"Well, their best is not good enough. They would have been happier for you to remain a widow for the rest of your life. They see you as free labour for the family business. Danny thinks they don't like him, and so do I. So, no thank you. We will not go begging for money from them. This is my mess, and I will sort it out."

"What do you mean 'your mess'? None of this is your fault. It's just bad luck."

"That is where you're wrong. We can't report the guitar stolen because that's how I got it. I stole it." Billy said, sobbing out loud.

Jing looked utterly mystified. "What do you mean? Explain."

"I stole that guitar while drunk one night almost forty years ago. I was just a stupid kid, like Danny."

Jing was shocked. "So that guitar that's just been stolen had already been stolen by you? Stolen from who? Where?"

Billy hesitated but finally answered, "From Jimi Hendrix."

"Oh, now I know you are kidding. Or else you have been drinking again. Or gone mad."

Billy wiped away his tears with his sleeve.

"In 1967, Jimi played one gig in Darlington, and I went along. That night, his black Stratocaster went missing, and it was never seen again. That's because it was inside a plastic bag, hidden in the pigeon loft at my parents until last year."

"You went to a concert where you stole a guitar from one of the most famous rock stars who ever lived, walked home with it and no one noticed?" Jing sounded unconvinced.

"That's about it. Except Jimi wasn't that famous then. I had never heard of him, nor had most of the other people I knew. I only went to the gig because some mates asked me to. In those days, no one ever asked me to go anywhere."

"You say you got drunk, and then what happened?"

"I can't remember much. I ended up outside on a side street, and the guitar was lying there next to me. I didn't put it there or know how it got there. But I was sure I would be accused of stealing it if I was found with it. So, I picked it up and ran for my life. It was late, dark, and raining. We only lived five minutes away.

"And no one witnessed this?"

"It was late on a dark and rainy mid-week night in the middle of winter. There was no one around other than those inside watching Jimi. I'm sure no one saw me because no one ever asked me about the guitar. The theft was in the papers the next day. If anyone had seen me running to our house, the police would have been around that very day. My unintentional crime seemed to have gone completely undetected."

"Why did you not just report it the following day? You could have returned it and explained that you found it and took it for safekeeping?"

"My parents had gone to stay in my uncle's caravan in Richmond. I was supposed to be at home house-sitting. I had no intention of explaining all this to my mother and father when they returned, or of being arrested for theft. I tried to forget about it and did so for nearly forty years."

Jing started to understand why the guitar had suddenly surfaced after all that time. "And then Danny wanted a guitar that we couldn't afford."

"Exactly. So, this is my mess, you see."

**CHAPTER TWELVE**

Billy had phoned Chris to tell him what had happened and to say there was no point driving over for their scheduled lesson as there was no Stratocaster to play on. Despite this, Chris said he would come and see if he could cheer Danny up. Billy told him he was wasting his time, but the musician insisted on coming anyway. "There'll be no charge. It's a personal mission," he added, doubting that his wife would see it quite the same way.

Chris rang the doorbell with his weak forefinger. His good left hand was carrying a battered guitar case. Billy welcomed him in and, pointing to the case, asked, "What have we here?"

"It's my Gibson Les Paul. It's supposed to have belonged to Bernie Marsden of Whitesnake, but sadly, I have no proof of that. It's beautiful. A classic. It's worth a few quid and it's the only pension planning I ever did."

"And you'll let Danny use it during your lessons? That's extremely kind of you."

"I was thinking more of an indefinite loan. Until you find Danny's Stratocaster, or he's made enough money from playing to buy another."

Billy was almost moved to tears by the generosity of this gesture, but from experience, he also knew better than to expect Danny's reaction to be the same.

"You've seen enough of Danny to know that there is nothing he likes less than change to his routines."

"Oh yes, I know. That one time, I had been to a friend's funeral and turned up all dressed in black, and he freaked out. You'd think he'd seen the Devil himself. I had to go back home and change into my usual denim before he would let me into his room. So, don't worry. I have a plan that might work.

Chris entered Danny's room without the guitar and told him how sorry he was about the theft of the Strat. He told him that he was sure it would turn up soon.

"I know we can't have a lesson until it's found, but in the meantime, I have a favour to ask you, Danny," Chris told him about his Gibson Les Paul and how he had acquired it from one of Whitesnake's roadies. On his laptop, he showed a video of Bernie Marsden playing a Les Paul on the track *Fool For Your Loving*. "If I ever find proof that this is the same guitar, it'll be worth a great deal of money."

Danny said nothing but had been distracted by the guitar playing on the video and appeared interested in the story.

"The Les Paul has been in its case since my accident. It has a broken string, and I can't replace it and re-tune it with my useless fingers. Would you do it for me?"

After a pause, Danny nodded slowly.

Chris stepped out into the corridor and retrieved the guitar case.

Within a minute or two, Danny had replaced the string with one Chris had in the case and re-tuned the guitar. He paused, holding the guitar, his left hand on the frets and his right hovering over the pickup. He looked up at Chris, who nodded, and Danny started to play *Hey Joe*.

A few bars into the song, Danny suddenly stopped. He returned the Les Paul to Chris and said, "There you are. Good as new."

"Don't you want to play some more?" Chris asked, looking dejected.

"No thanks. It's not the same. It's your guitar. I want my Strat back and I don't understand why Dad won't call the police."

"Unfortunately, I agree with your dad. The police are unlikely to look very hard for it. That guitar would be difficult to identify and too easy to sell for cash."

"That's crap. I could identify it in a moment. It's got lots of little marks on the neck. I'd know it anywhere."

"Sadly, Danny, by now, it will have been fenced to someone who probably can't play a note. It will become an ornament propped up in a corner of some music nerd's bedroom."

This prognosis was not what Danny wanted to hear. He spun around and threw himself face down on the bed, covering his ears with his hands and shaking his head violently.

"Look," Chris added. "If your guitar turns up, you manage to get a replacement, or you decide that you'd like to play this one for the competition, let me know.

I'd be more than happy to drive you guys to London, if you'd like me to."

But Danny didn't make a sound and Chris left the room.

"That went well, then," Billy observed sarcastically.

"Sorry. I tried."

"We know, and we really appreciate it."

Chris realised that he could no longer put off telling Billy the real reason for his coming over. "I'm sorry to be the bearer of more bad news, and I know the timing could not be worse, but I can't come over here anymore."

Billy looked stunned.

"My old car failed its MOT, which would cost nearly a thousand pounds to fix. I simply don't have that kind of money and nor am I likely to any time soon. I'm sorry, Billy, but I just can't get here for Danny's lessons."

Billy told him he understood and thanked him for everything he had done.

Danny was inconsolable. He went back into his shell, staying in his room most of the time he was at home. Not even Kat was allowed into whatever corner of his mind he had gone to hide in. She had been trying anything she could to raise money from school friends to fund the band's trip to London. Since hearing about the theft of his guitar, plenty of people had been willing to help, and all kinds of fundraising events had been planned. Danny should have been flattered and encouraged, but he was not interested.

They were already several days closer to the date. Still, Li was reluctant to tell the competition organisers they were unlikely to attend. She clung to the unlikely possibility that Danny's guitar might suddenly materialise out of thin air. She even dreamed about it emerging from the water-filled quarry near the school, like King Arthur's Excalibur from the lake.

**CHAPTER THIRTEEN**

The school caretaker had been undertaking his own investigation. A rock music fan himself, he had been the one to suggest the band use the music room to rehearse and to leave their instruments there. He also locked up the school after they were finished, sometimes indulging in a personal fantasy by holding the guitars and pretending to play. So he felt more than a little guilty about what had happened to Danny's Strat.

Several other after-school activities went on each evening, so plenty of people milled around the corridors after regular lessons. The CCTV covered mainly the outside areas. Car parks, entrances and potential smoking and snogging areas were all covered, but only the reception, offices, and a few main corridors, internally.

With an intimate understanding of the layout, the caretaker narrowed down the possible routes to and from the music rooms with camera coverage. There were only two corridors and a fire exit, although there could also be routes to other parts of the building. This ruled out as many as ninety per cent of the people in the building. Most were sports classes, and those attending them had no reason to be in that part of the school.

The amateur detective rationalised that with pupils ranging from eleven to seventeen, it was most likely to be those at the higher end of that range who would steal a guitar. Luckily, the other activities taking place in the accessible rooms were a beginner's cookery course, mainly attended by first-year pupils, and a life drawing class, which only had three girls signed up. That left only about a dozen older teenagers who could be seen entering and leaving this part of the building between the rehearsal finishing and when he locked up.

He asked the school's head of music to go through the images with him to find out more about those identified as potential suspects. When they reached the third pupil to appear on the recordings, the teacher said, "Ah. Jason Smith-Booth. Wanna-be rock guitar player. He's got the image and all the band t-shirts but none of the skill and is too lazy to practice. I recall that he wanted to join Danny's band, but they turned him down. Apparently, Danny wasn't very subtle about it. In front of several of their peers, including some girls, Danny is supposed to have told Jason that he was 'a crap guitar player' and just walked away without so much as looking back."

"I can see that wouldn't go down very well," the caretaker said.

"I think he might be our best suspect. But if Jason took it, why is he seen leaving ten minutes later and not carrying a guitar?"

"Still, he seems to have a strong motive and the opportunity," the caretaker said.

"As I'm not teaching staff, would you speak to the headmaster about the possibility of us having a word with him?"

When Jason was summoned to attend a meeting in the music room after school the following day and provided a letter for him to take home to his parents, inviting them to attend, Jason guessed what was coming. Someone must have found the Stratocaster. He knew his prints and possibly his DNA would be on the guitar. After trying but failing to figure a way out of the hole he had dug for himself, he had no choice but to confess to his father and hope he could save him. His dad asked about CCTV, and then Jason realised he had not even thought of that. The next morning, he confirmed that his father, who was a lawyer, would also be coming to the meeting.

At 4.30 pm, the five took seats arranged roughly in a circle in the centre of the music room. Jason's father was a tall, robust individual whose physique suggested he might have played rugby as a younger man, and wore what was clearly an expensive suit. The Headmaster began, "You know that a guitar left in this room has gone missing?" Everyone nodded. "CCTV places you, Jason," he continued, "as one of a handful of people in this area of the building at that time. And yet, on checking the timetables, I see that you were the only one with no classes here and, therefore, no reason to be in school. So, why were you there, Jason?"

At this point, Jason's father spoke. "Firstly, all of this is circumstantial and proves nothing. This meeting appears to be informal as it is not being recorded or minuted. Is that correct, Headmaster?"

"At the moment, this is all off the record. However, if any criminal activity is revealed, I must consider escalating the matter. But for now, we can talk freely."

"It's good that you mention criminal activity because, as I'm sure you are aware, that is my area of expertise. The law defines theft as the dishonest appropriation of property belonging to another with the intention of depriving the other of it permanently. This usually involves physically taking something away from its owner to keep or sell. Can we agree on this as a general definition?"

No one disagreed, though the headmaster looked a little bemused. "The other thing I think we can probably all agree on is that Jason here is an idiot."

They all smiled, but the music teacher could not help guffawing aloud. Again no one disagreed.

The lawyer continued, "Apart from Jason, who has yet to do anything useful with his life, the rest of us are busy people with work to get on with. My meter is running, and my son cannot afford my rates. So, I will propose the following summary of where we are. If the accepted definition of theft had not been met and this meeting is off the record, then the guitar's rediscovery would presumably end the matter. Jason could leave the school in three months after his examinations with no written record of his stupidity going with him."

There was general nodding among the adults. His father looked at Jason and nodded. The young man climbed up on a table and reached up with both arms to remove a large white tile from the suspended ceiling. In the void, and now visible to all in the room, was the neck of an electric guitar. With some manoeuvring, Jason carefully slid the instrument out of its hiding place, along with a surprising amount of dust that caused Jason to cough. The boy handed the guitar to his father, who gave it to the Principal.

"I think we all know why Jason did this," Jason's father said. "It was a terrible misjudgement and disproportionate overreaction driven by inferior motives. But significantly, it does not amount to theft. Clearly, he did not intend to deprive the owner of it permanently. He certainly intended to punish Danny by temporarily depriving him of it, but not to keep or sell it. Therefore, by our agreed definition, it is not theft."

The lawyer paused to let these words sink in as he would in a jury trial.

"Finally, we need to deal with the acknowledged temporary loss of the use of the instrument and any distress that has caused. I understand from Jason's sister that the owner of this guitar and his band have been invited to play in a competition in London but are struggling to raise the cost of expenses. The firm where I am a partner has a fund to support community causes, which seems like a particularly good one to me. Headmaster, if you email me telling me who to make the payment to, my firm will cover three hundred pounds of their expenses."

The Headmaster fully understood what was taking place and that the power dynamic had shifted.

"Given your comparison with what would otherwise be civil litigation, I understand that, at this point, it is customary for there to be some negotiation between those representing the opposing parties. Allowing for Danny's somewhat unusual personal circumstances, the level of distress for him and his family has been considerably greater than might otherwise have been the case. Six hundred pounds would seem to be a more appropriate figure in compensation."

Jason's father forced a smile with pursed lips. "As you say, Headmaster, these are special circumstances. Send me the bank details, and six hundred pounds will be paid without delay."

There were smiles all around, except for Jason, who seemed extremely cross.

Looking slightly more relaxed than when he had arrived, the lawyer added, "In that case, I think our business here is concluded, and we bid you good day. Jason has a considerable amount of gardening and car washing to do."

Jason left the room, nudged by his father, leaving behind a much-relieved group whose faith in human nature was somewhat restored.

"Who is going to call Danny's family?" the caretaker asked.

"I suggest you take the guitar around to his house. It was your work that led to its recovery."

**CHAPTER FOURTEEN**

At school, the excitement grew as the competition drew closer. However, Danny and his family all harboured unspoken reservations about his first trip away from home without his parents.

"It's only one night," Billy assured his wife. "And Chris will be there with them all the time. He loves Chris." Billy had revelled in the joy of being able to call Chris and tell him Danny's Stratocaster had been recovered, and that he would be thrilled to drive them to London. Chris, it seemed, already had an idea that would make the trip a real event for them all.

Jing forced a smile, "I know you are right. Our bird must fly solo sometime."

Later that day, Chris called with the astonishing news that a song he had co-written twenty years earlier had been included in a Hollywood movie that was to be released, complete with a famous cast and Oscar-winning director.

"I opened the letter, and a cheque for fifteen grand fell out. And I'm told there's more to come as the movie rolls out worldwide and eventually onto streaming channels. It's like the pension I thought I'd never have, "Chris said with a grin.

Almost speechless, Billy asked, "But why you? Why now, after all these years?"

"Well, the song always had a great riff, but apparently, the lyric clinched it. The song was about the attraction to young lovers of American-style bench seats in sixties cars. I called it Bench Seat Love. It was all references to stick-shift gears and no hand-brake levers. You get the idea."

Billy pointed out that Chris had always told him that nothing they ever recorded sold any records. "It sold less than a hundred copies, mainly to family and friends. It bombed, and the record company dropped us. The movie people found it by searching a digital music archive using keywords. It just fitted perfectly with a major scene in the movie. They have remixed the song and embellished it using modern techniques. However, essentially, it's still half my song, backing vocal and lead guitar."

"That must take the financial pressure off you at home. Is your wife pleased?"

"She left me four weeks ago for a car dealer she met at the spray tanning shop. She said she was sick of my coming here to play at being a rock star instead of getting a proper job to pay the bills. She packed her bags and ran off with him to his villa in Portugal. So, no, I'm not planning to share my good news with her."

Chris explained that this was not the entire reason for the phone call. He wanted to spend a little of his good fortune on extending Danny's band's trip to the competition. He argued that they needed to be fully immersed in the Jimi Hendrix Experience to play their best for the competition. Chris was proposing that they retrace the mini tour that Jimi and his band made, which brought them to Darlington and then back to London in 1967.

"If they can visit the places Jimi played and talk to people who actually saw him, Danny and the others will better understand the difficulties musicians experienced back then. All the challenges Jimi had to overcome to achieve his success should motivate them to try harder for their own."

Billy sensed that there was perhaps another reason why Chris wanted to do this. Danny's band had already become Chris's way to continue living out his own musical dreams. Now, he had unexpectedly achieved some recognition of his skills, and felt empowered to push Danny a little further toward his dream. "We can make this a road trip of inspiration. It might just make the difference between winning and losing this competition. Also, these teenagers are growing up. It might be time for a small taste of freedom."

"And you'll be back on the road with a rock band, all-be-it as their tour manager," Billy observed wryly.

"Well, that's true. It would be nice to escape Middlesbrough's smoky skyline for a few days. Chris Rea only romanticises about the factory chimneys and smog in his songs because he doesn't have to live amongst them."

After some negotiations about the length of the trip and assurances about sleeping arrangements, both sets of parents agreed to an extension for a day or possibly two at most. They would travel to London via

Ilkley and Leeds, staying overnight in a borrowed tour bus on Chris's friend's farm in the Peak District.

Chris had called in a favour from what was the Northeast's best-known touring band. They were a trio of older musicians who had all previously been members of successful pop chart bands. One had left his group because they'd all fallen out and could no longer work together. One had been kicked out of his band for having an affair with the drummer's wife. The third had saved plenty of money from his career and still had songwriting royalties coming in. He just wanted to choose when and where he played and could afford to be picky. His former bandmates had not been so lucky. Neither had they written any revenue-earning hits, so they needed to play live constantly to make ends meet.

The collective music pedigrees of the trio made them an extremely popular band, particularly in northern European countries. They filled venues with several thousand fans of each or all of their collective bands. It was easy, pleasant, and well-paid work, with no pressure, no long-haul flights or months spent on the road. Pete had bought a large American camper van and had it converted to carry the band's minimal equipment and sleep all of them plus a driver-cum-roadie in reasonable comfort.

Chris had told Pete, their band leader, the story of Danny and his band and he immediately agreed to help. The trio were taking a couple of weeks off following an extended tour of northern Europe. Providing he paid for insurance, Chris could use their customised vehicle, which had sleeping bunks for six people. Pete also put fancy guitar peddles, cables, and even a couple of really good amplifiers in the hold to supplement the young band's meagre kit. With Danny's guitar back in his hands, the newly christened Spirit of Jimi practised as they had never before to prepare for the competition.

**CHAPTER FIFTEEN**

Kat and Li had got together with their schoolmates in art technology classes to design and make signs to go above the front and rear windscreens of the bus, which read, 'Spirit of Jimi – on tour'. In addition to the six hundred pounds from the law firm, school friends had raised another three hundred and fifty through various sponsored events. With almost a thousand-pound budget, they could cover the fuel for the bus, all their meals, and have one night in a hotel before the concert.

Jing ensured Danny had all his favourite t-shirts and the other clothes he loved. She had to wash and rotate these items regularly because her son was reluctant to adopt anything new. All breaks in routine unsettled Danny. He found comfort in the familiar, so even his usual bedding and duvet were placed on one of the bus's bunk beds and a poster of Jimi from his bedroom was taped to the panel above where he would sleep.

Jing's parents were going to pay for Billy and her to travel by train and stay overnight at a hotel in London, much to Billy's embarrassment after what he had said about their meanness.

Before the trip, Kat bleached her previously pink hair almost white, and after two years, it had been time for the metal braces to come off her teeth. She even allowed her mum to apply a little make-up, though she was worried about how Danny might react to these changes. Still, she felt confident about their relationship and decided to risk it. When she saw the new Kat, her mother wept.

"You are my beautiful angel. I only wish your father were alive to see you," she said and hugged her daughter so close she could hardly breathe.

"He can see me, mum. I talk to him sometimes and I feel like he's watching."

Danny's reaction took time. Kat thought he looked shocked to the core; this time, it was her turn to cry. Realising that it was his lack of reaction that was upsetting her, he hugged her tightly. Danny had never been so spontaneous with her or held her like that.

"You look beautiful. Like an angel," he mumbled close to Kat's ear.

"That's exactly what my mum said," she said, laughing through the tears.

"Well, we're both right. You really are."

Danny had never used such tender words to Kat. She had always seen his affection in his eyes, but this was the first time he had ever articulated his feelings. It felt good. Very good indeed.

Without planning to, Kat kissed Danny. Unnerved, at first, he pulled away. Then realising how good it felt, pulled her back, and returned the kiss, lingering longer this time.

**CHAPTER SIXTEEN**

Danny and Li waved excitedly from the rear window as the bus pulled away. Billy wondered if he had done the right thing. Was he setting his vulnerable son up for a fall from which his confidence might never recover? Unearthing his twenty-year-old secret may have given Danny an outlet for his emotions, but there were less risky ways to have done that.

If he had been smarter or worked harder, he might have been able to afford better help for Danny. Billy had taken the first job he was offered and never tried to improve his position. As a young, single man, what had seemed easy, safe, and unchallenging now looked like a complete cop-out of responsibility.

In many ways, Billy recognised parts of Danny in himself. He, too, did not like change and was comfortable with the familiar. He had never had ambitions to travel, excel at sport or play a musical instrument. The idea of being anyone's boss or running his own company would have been unthinkable. Only now did he recognise that these decisions had influenced his children's lives. Not just Danny's, but also Li's childhoods had been compromised by their underprivileged circumstances.

With tears in his eyes for the second time in a week, he turned to Jing. "I've failed them both."

"Billy, what on earth do you mean? This competition is their chance of some success. You should be crying with joy."

"In a way, I am, but this throw of the dice is probably their only chance. If I had been a more successful father and earned more, they would not be relying upon what is at best a long shot."

Jing hugged her husband. "Billy, you have been a wonderful father. Unlike many, your job has allowed you to spend time with the children. And you gave them quality time; playing with them, gardening, trying to help them with their homework. You didn't go to the golf course, football, or fishing like many fathers do to get out of child-rearing. Those memories are far more valuable than being in front of a TV screen or giving them expensive toys. Those things would all have been forgotten by now. You were there when they stumbled. You hugged them when they cried. And they love you even more as a result."

Billy seemed somewhat reassured but added, "I always felt haunted by that bloody guitar. The guilt of it hung over me like a cloud. Now, at least, it might finally do some good."

"You knew you might be risking your freedom by bringing that guitar out of hiding. That was a hell of a risk to take, even for your son. But you found that guitar in the street. You didn't take it from its owner or even remove it from the building. Someone surely would have stolen it if it had been left where you found it. Even in your drunken state, you probably knew it needed to be put in a safe place. It's not your fault that its owner didn't value it enough to report it stolen. Even if you'd taken it to the police station, the chances are that they would have just placed it in lost property. Eventually, after several weeks unclaimed, they would have returned it to the finder. The outcome might have been the same."

"But it's probably worth much more money now," Billy protested.

"No one, including you, knew that then. You didn't take it home because it was valuable or even because you wanted to play it. The Billy I know has never taken anything that was not his. I think you took it home because you knew it was at risk, but then you didn't know how you would explain having it to your parents. You didn't steal it because you didn't profit from it in any way.

Within days of the Darlington concert, *Hey Joe* went into the top ten and Jimi's fortunes were transformed. That guitar's value quickly became small change to him. A few years later, he was dead, and only then did anyone start to want Jimi's belongings, and prices went crazy. How could you have possibly known any of that would happen?"

"I am sorry, but I can't help but feel I should have handled it better," Billy insisted.

"By doing what exactly? I'm sorry if this sounds selfish, Billy, but from my point of view, it has been a gift from Jimi up in heaven. None of this could have happened had it not been for the magic that guitar has brought into our lives."

**CHAPTER SEVENTEEN**

When the tour bus left Darlington, Chris began his history lesson on life on the road for bands when he started. He explained that a decade before his first outing, Jimi Hendrix would have had an even tougher experience travelling between gigs.

"This is the absolute lap of luxury compared to how most bands travelled back then. Even ten years after Jimi, we were packed into small vans, which were always old and noisy. They broke down regularly and often smelled very bad. Commercial vehicles always had a strong odour of whatever they had carried during their previous working lives – meat, fish, engine oil - you name it. Former milk vans were the worst."

"But why? Milk is not especially smelly," Li pointed out.

"Not when it's fresh. But when the bottles get dropped, it runs into the seams of the floor, where it congeals and festers until it smells like the worst cheese gone off. And, if money was tight or it got too late, they often slept in the van, sleeping bags stretched out on amplifiers and across the bench seat at the front. In summer, even up on the roof. There were no Travel Lodges, motorway services, McDonalds, or Costa Coffee shops. Laybys were toilets; catering was usually strong tea and bacon sandwiches from a converted caravan by the side of the road."

The teenagers all smiled at the thought of a group of grown men living out of a van that smelled of stale milk.

"That's why all old rockers smell of patchouli oil. It's to hide the eau-de-van." Eventually, they all got Chris's joke and simulated laughter. They were enjoying the trip. Being treated like equals and having grown-up conversations with an adult was liberating.

As they joined the A1 heading south, Chris told them there would have been no motorway north of Leeds in 1967. The old road wound between towns and through villages, making journey times twice as long as today.

"In the pre-sat nav world, we relied on printed paper maps to find the way between places." Chris extracted an old AA Road Atlas from 1985 from the pocket in the door and passed it to Danny.

"Find me the best way to Ilkley please, Danny."

Opening the book with over two hundred pages, each containing a colour-coded map, he had no idea where to start. He got out his iPhone, typed the keypad, and a digital voice offered directions to Ilkley.

Chris laughed, "Oh, I'm glad you reminded me. The phones were a bit different, too. Public pay phones were in red painted metal boxes by the side of public roads."

Danny said, "The old phone box is blue in Doctor Who."

"Ah, that's a phone box only for the Police to use because they also had no wireless communications. The public ones were red. A village might have one to itself. In towns, they were shared by neighbourhoods, and there was sometimes a queue to use them. They usually stank of urine, the single light bulb had as often as not been stolen, and you needed the right coins to put in the slots to make it work. Two pence minimum, as I recall. But if you wanted to contact the venue where you were due to play to say you had broken down and would arrive late, that was the only way."

"No email?" Li asked.

"No text messages, WhatsApp, or Messenger either. Just letters and phone boxes. Mail required pen and paper, plus a postage stamp on an envelope," Chris confirmed, to her astonishment.

"This was also before voicemail. So, if no one answered, you had to drive on and wait to find another phone to try again and hope someone picked up the receiver."

Chris asked them to imagine the reaction Jimi received when he turned up in provincial northern towns, where people of colour were rare and Americans even rarer. A tall, skinny black guy with long, unkempt hair wearing skintight flared trousers and a purple silk shirt under a gold braided jacket must have looked like he had just beamed in from outer space.

"Take me to your leader," Danny mimicked, remembering the line from old Dr Who episodes he'd seen.

It was Chris's turn to laugh out loud as they all joined in.

"He must have been lonely so far away from home?" Li speculated, changing the subject back to Jimi.

"You're probably right, but he met a girl in London soon after he arrived, and they were close for most of the next few years. She often travelled with him. She was certainly with him in Darlington that night your dad saw him."

There was silence and astonishment on the faces of the teenagers.

"Our dad saw Jimi Hendrix play in Darlington? No. You must be mistaken. He would have said."

"I don't think I'm mistaken. The guy who put your father in touch with me about your guitar lessons told me they went to the gig together. Considering what has happened since, I can't imagine why he hasn't mentioned it."

Danny looked at Li, shaking his head in disbelief. Chris was beginning to suspect that there must be some reason why Billy had kept this a secret, but had no idea what it might be. He decided it might be a good idea to change the subject.

"After Darlington, Jimi went to play at the Club a'Gogo in Newcastle before heading back to Yorkshire following the route we are taking today. His manager, Chas, had booked him a gig at the Troutbeck Hotel in Ilkley. His fame must have spread by then because Chas negotiated a twenty per cent increase in their fee up to a princely ninety pounds for the night."

"No way," Danny exclaimed. "Jimi Hendrix played in my hometown for seventy-five quid."

"It's true. Seventy-five pounds was in the contract, plus a promise of two rounds of drinks from the organiser. Tickets were sold at ten shillings, the equivalent of fifty pence today."

Danny's speedy mental arithmetic informed him, "They needed to sell a hundred and eighty tickets just to pay the band."

"A hundred tickets seemed an optimistic expectation when they booked him, but Jimi's appearance on national TV in December ensured they sold more than enough to cover their costs by the second of February. The story goes that, realising he could now command a higher fee at bigger venues,

Chas Chandler had offered the Darlington organiser a substantial profit on the agreed fifty-pound fee if they let Jimi out of his contractual agreement. As we now know, they declined the offer because the gig went ahead as planned, but it cost Jimi a guitar."

The connection between the young band and the artist who had inspired them was developing. From purely a two-dimensional image and sound, Chris's talks made Jimi flesh and bone again. He was becoming a real person to them, but one living in a time very different from today. Someone with all the hopes and fears of an insecure foreigner who was yet to become rich and famous. A lonely young man in a very strange place, up until this point, scratching an existence as best he could. Li, in particular, began to feel really sorry for him.

"The poor guy must have been terrified. What if things hadn't worked out? They could turn up to play, and no one turn up to see them. They might not get paid. He could easily have found himself broke, homeless, and thousands of miles from home and whatever family he had left."

"And don't forget the racial prejudice. Black faces were few and far between north of Leeds. Most Northerners were not very worldly or well-travelled. They didn't like what they didn't understand. All of which must have motivated Jimi to be exceptional to win them over," Chris pointed out.

Danny saw it slightly differently. "If he was that scared, he could have played safe. Jimi was a good enough guitarist to play how all the others did but just do it better. He did not have to take risks, but that's exactly what he did. He played stuff no one had heard before in a way they'd never seen. And I heard that not everyone got him at first."

"It didn't always go down well. Only a few people turned up at one of the places we will be visiting, and not all of those who did go were impressed. One called him "shit" and asked for his money back. You make a good point, Danny; he could have trotted out all the old R&B classics, and they would still have loved him just for his style and skill. But that wasn't Jimi. He only did things his way."

**CHAPTER EIGHTEEN**

As the bus approached Ilkley, the old town was bathed in late morning sunshine. Undulating terraces of stout granite houses followed the contours of the hills until they reached green pastures where lines of drystone walls outlined a landscape dotted with white sheep.

Chris tried to put on a Yorkshire accent, "Welcome to God's country, as they call it around here."

"Why do they call it God's country, Chris? And whose God are they referring to?" Li asked in all innocence.

"When they coined that phrase, there was only one God in Yorkshire and a single cricket team you could support. When textiles and the Industrial Revolution made this one of the richest counties in England, there were only white faces around here. Now, there are as many mosque minarets as church spires, and the former are better attended. For test matches at Headingly, Indian and Pakistan supporters might outnumber England's two-to-one. Times have changed."

Chris explained that the building they were to visit had once been The Troutbeck Hotel, complete with a restaurant, bars, and a concert room. With a capacity of two hundred and fifty people, the ballroom was often hired out for parties and gigs like Jimi's. Since then, the hotel has been converted into a retirement home.

"You're taking a rock band on tour to an old people's home?" Danny questioned.

"I'm taking you to the scene of one of Jimi's best-attended but scariest gigs on his earliest tour. It might be all peace and serenity now, but in 1967 a near riot occurred here in Ilkley."

Now, the teenagers were intrigued. Chris explained that he had phoned ahead to the home and been given permission to show them the room where Jimi had played. The facility's manager had also told him that one of their residents had been at the concert and would enjoy telling anyone who would listen about her experiences that night.

"She must be very, very old?" Li said.

"Not so old. Seventy-five, to be precise," Chris corrected.

"Making her nineteen in 1967," Danny added before anyone else could work it out. Just six years younger than Jimi was at that time.

When the bus pulled into the car park of the Troutbeck Residential Home, there was an old lady in a wheelchair waiting with a younger woman.

"Welcome to Troutbeck." the older lady said with the confident voice of someone half her age. "My name is Cynthia Coleman, but everyone always called me Cynth."

Chris, who had previously spoken to both women on the phone, bent down to hug Cynth. With less self-assurance, the teenagers introduced themselves.

"Let's start the tour because lunch is served here at noon on the dot. Otherwise, there will be a bigger riot than when Jimi played here."

Cynth talked as they made their way along floral wallpapered corridors in single file, telling them that the ticket that night had cost the equivalent of a day's wage.

"That's a lot for a band we hadn't heard much of. All there was to go on was the one single that was climbing the charts and another track they'd played on a TV program. What we heard was strange and frankly, Jimi looked terrifying. Like nothing we had ever seen in Yorkshire. I suspect most, like me, came out of curiosity because he'd been on the telly rather than because we were fans."

When they reached the room where the concert had been, they found it empty of furniture. It had a high ceiling and a wooden parquet floor with a raised stage at one end. The care worker pushing Cynth told them, "We rarely use this room now. It's too big and so expensive to heat."

"That night, the agent who had booked it sold almost four times more tickets than the room was licensed for. People had come from all over Yorkshire. We all got in, but it was packed, and the crush made it feel intimidating. But it was also exciting. Everyone had got dressed up in their best outfits and had their hair done," Cynth added with a twinkle in her eye

"The band looked so exotic, with their long hair and strange clothes. We thought we were dressed fashionably but looked boring compared to Jimi and the band. I have a photograph of my friend and me taken earlier that night before we left home."

"You didn't take any photos at the gig?" Li asked.

Chris interjected. "There were no phone cameras in those days. Photographs required expensive rolls of film and so each shot was precious. Nighttime photos needed a flash, and not all household cameras had that facility."

Cynth was nodding in agreement. "That's right. My mum took these on the doorstep of our house before we got the bus here. If Dad had been home from work, I doubt he would have let us go out dressed like this. Our skirts were a bit short."

She handed Li the black and white prints, who then passed them to Danny and the others. They showed two attractive teenagers wearing similar printed shift dresses that stopped well above the knee. The girls, one blonde and the other dark had their hair cut on the bias, as Li recalled seeing on images of fashion models from the sixties. They glanced at Cynth in her wheelchair and then back at the photo, trying to reconcile the difference fifty-plus years had made.

The pensioner told them how Jimi had been just two numbers into his show when several uniformed police entered the room and climbed onto the stage.

"One located the power source for the equipment and turned it off. Presumably, the senior officer in his peaked cap and braided shoulders had spoken to Jimi, who looked completely calm and, without fuss, consented to the police's request to leave the stage. That was in stark contrast to the crowd which quickly became an angry mob. Having paid what they thought was a lot of money, only hearing two songs felt like a con. No one mentioned offering a refund. The police just started pushing everyone out of the room. My friend and I were a bit scared. We edged toward the back of the room and left by a fire exit someone had opened."

Cynth told them that the next day, the event was reported in the Yorkshire Post as a near riot. Chairs were thrown onto the stage, paintings ripped from the walls, and fighting broke out between the officers, and some ticket holders demanding their money back. Jimi, the band, and the promoter ran out through the same fire door and left the police to deal with the furious mob.

"There we were, standing around outside with Jimi and the band, Chas Chandler, and a man I vaguely recognised from the Ilkley pub scene, who must have been the promoter. To this day, it was simultaneously the most exciting and terrifying event of my life. But I was as close to Jimi as I am to you now, and something about him exuded star quality. I'll never forget it."

Cynth looked suddenly sad but then added, "He had kind, dreamy eyes."

Li, listening intently, said, "Wow, seeing Jim Hendrix in front of a crowd of a couple of hundred people in a small town hotel ballroom is the equivalent today of Taylor Swift playing live at our school prom."

Suddenly excited and animated, Cynth added, "Oh, I almost forgot. A few weeks later, I met a girl at a wedding who said that she had been at Harry Ramsden's fish shop that same night when Jimi and the band rolled up in an old van. Someone recognised him, and he chatted with the people in the queue while patiently waiting his turn. This girl did not have any paper, so she asked Jimi to sign his autograph on her fish 'n' chip wrapper, which he did and gave her a little peck on the cheek. She said he was lovely but smelled funny."

"That'll have been the marijuana," Chris whispered to Danny.

"Or a milk van," Danny quipped back at him.

They thanked Cynth and her carer, and said their goodbyes before returning to the bus.

"What do you think about Jimi now that you've talked to people who met him?"

Li looked at the others, seeking affirmation and answered, "I think we all assumed he was a rebel. A drug-using, tough guy. Someone you would want to avoid, other than when he was onstage."

The others all nodded, and Chris agreed. "I think that was most people's view."

"But now I see a quiet, vulnerable guy who had a lot to be angry about, yet wasn't," Li said with genuine emotion.

Danny added, "People seemed to like him as a man. Not just a musician. He was kind to people he'd never met and didn't flaunt his fame or eventual wealth."

Tom chipped in, "I would have expected him to resist the police getting him offstage like that in Ilkley, but he didn't. I would have been seething if that had happened to us!"

"That's drummers for you. Always troublemakers," Chris joked.

**CHAPTER NINETEEN**

Although Danny had only been away from home for a few hours, he was beginning to feel a little bewildered. He had visited new places before but always with one or both of his parents. This trip with his peers, whilst exciting, left him feeling a little out of his depth. He was experiencing an unfamiliar sensation of longing, but it was not for his mum and dad.

Danny realised that it was Kat who occupied all his thoughts. The vision of her face and the taste of her lips from the night before still lingered, and he missed her terribly. An ache had developed in his stomach that, even though it made no sense, Danny was sure was somehow connected. Li could see her brother looking anxious, and that he had not spoken to anyone in a while.

"You OK, Dan?" she asked.

Deep in his thoughts, Danny didn't answer.

"Hey, little brother. What's up?"

Snapping out of his daydream, Danny finally spoke. "Would anyone have minded if Kat had come with us?"

The question surprised Li, but she quickly told him that she would not have objected if she been asked. "We all like Kat, and you are more relaxed when she's around. Even though you ignore her most of the time, she seems to enjoy being with the band, and for some strange reason, she likes you."

Danny ignored his sibling's unflattering remarks, "I don't know why I didn't think of it before we left, but I could have asked her to come to London with us." Danny said, looking deflated.

Li said, "We're only going as far as Leeds this afternoon. It's only an hour from Darlington by train. If she misses you as much as you're missing her, she could meet us there this afternoon. If her mum will let her go on her own, that is. You had better ask Chris first, though. He has a schedule."

After several phone calls to Darlington and a conversation with Chris, Kat and her mum set off for Leeds.

Meanwhile, the tour bus made its way through North Leeds to the suburb of Chapeltown. In 1967, this area had become an enclave for Asian and

Caribbean immigrants. Members of the latter group congregated at the International Club to gamble, drink, and dance. The first-floor concert room was one of the few places in the North where reggae music was played live. Jimi had been booked to play there after the sold-out but disastrous event in Ilkley. Fortunately, before the Internet, bad news did not spread anything like as quickly, nor was it distorted quite as much by people to their own agendas.

Sadly, nothing was left of the International Club, but they had come to meet someone Chris had found who had once worked there as a doorman. In a café only a few hundred meters from the site of the former club, Adio, was serving teas, coffees, and Caribbean snacks. He had clearly been expecting the three teenagers and their driver, as his face lit up when they entered the café.

"Welcome to Adio's. You can keep your shoes on, but please leave your long faces and hang-ups outside," was the unusual greeting that awaited them. The proprietor was a mountain of a man with a badly broken nose, which sat uncomfortably on a gnarled complexion. Had it not been for the row of white teeth with several gold fillings revealed by his ear-to-ear smile, Adio would have been an intimidating figure. A younger woman appeared from the kitchen, allowing Adio to sit at a table with them.

"Hungry?" Adio asked.

They all looked to Chris for a lead but when he nodded, they also nodded enthusiastically. "Four bowls of souse and some Johnny cakes," Adio shouted toward the kitchen. "A beer for you, Chris?"

Chris shook his head. "Thanks, but I'm driving."

"OK, what can I tell you about Jimi at the International Club?"

Li was first to ask why so few people from an immigrant community went to see him.

"You think we like the same things because we have the same skin tone? If that were the case, the Irish Protestants would be having Catholics over for tea after church and Indians would be inviting Pakistanis around for a curry. Life is just not that simple, I'm afraid."

Li still looked puzzled.

Adio tried to explain. "Most people around here in those days were Asian or Caribbean. Neither culture shared anything much with the other, let alone with black Americans - especially not music. Add an instinctive wariness for anyone new and strange, like Jimi. And man, he certainly was strange."

"But surely you all faced racism to some extent?" asked Tom, who rarely contributed much to their discussions. "I would have thought that would have galvanised support for Jimi here in Leeds."

Adio sighed, "I guess you could say we were as racist as anyone he encountered. We harboured our own prejudices against Jimi's culture, which was as foreign to us as the Caribbean one was to the British. Fear of the unknown is a natural survival instinct as old as humanity. If in doubt, treat strange people, animals, or plants as a threat. Don't think white folk have a monopoly on racism."

Chris pointed out that almost all of Jimi's fans at that point were white middle-class Europeans with virtually nothing in common with him. In London, his initial successes had been in Belgravia and Chelsea, not

Notting Hill or the East End where most immigrants were living.

"Perhaps strange is what white teenagers were looking for," Danny added.

Li looked even more puzzled. "What do you mean by that?"

Uncharacteristically, Danny was forthright with his explanation. "These post-war teenagers were done with traditions. They despised the world their parents clung to. The Beatles had shown that radical changes were possible, and fun. The establishment and every parent would hate Jimi and everything he stood for, so the kids loved him. Whether they understood or liked his music was not the whole point."

"Wow. That's some heavy analysis, Danny. Where did that come from?"

Danny smiled fondly at his sister. "I might not talk much, but I read a bit and think quite a lot."

"I think Danny paints a pretty accurate picture of how things were then," Chris added.

Adio said, "Ska, rocksteady and reggae were the music played at our club. Although it also used guitars, it was much slower and more mellow. It was all about a bass rhythm that got people dancin'. Jimi's stuff, with its guitar solos, was more for sitting, smoking, and listening to. In Jamaica, people want to dance and feel that bass in their stomach as they move."

Adio explained that Jimi only got booked because his manager was a good salesperson. "He sold him as a cool black guy who had appeared on TV and would pull people into the club. And he was cheap. He failed to mention he was an American, played radical R&B, or that they were only a three-piece band."

"So, it was a disaster," Chris summarised, putting words in Adio's mouth.

"Not entirely," the former bouncer said, laughing. "There was some argument about the fee. But Chas Chandler was a big, tough Geordie and stood his ground. As a compromise, I suggested they take part payment in ganja. They agreed, but as they were used to paying London prices, I made a few quid on the deal. But that Jimi was a cool dude. Nothing much seemed to bother him. He played to twenty people as if it was two hundred. Some of the audience mocked him, but he ignored them, turned his back to them and played harder and louder. Some balls that guy had."

Danny's band finished their spicy Caribbean lunch, thanked Adio and went on their way, a little wiser about Jimi.

**CHAPTER TWENTY**

From Chapeltown, the group headed into central Leeds. Chris had asked the group if they minded if he visited an old friend who had a shop in the Victoria Quarter. The architecturally flamboyant, covered arcade had once been the home only to small independent shops. In recent years, it had been restored, rents had risen, and it was becoming a gentrified hub for designer labels, cafes, and bakers of expensive pastries. Although a few independent stores hung on to old leases, including Bootleggers. 'Soles and Heels for Rock Royalty' proclaimed their window graphics.

Tony, the owner, was standing in the open doorway when Chris and the three teenagers appeared. Danny had his guitar in a canvas case on his back. Since the incident with Jason, he'd sworn he would not let it out of sight again.

"Bloody Hell. Those can't be your kids?" Tony said, looking astonished while holding out both arms in a warm Northern greeting. "No, not mine," Chris replied, hugging his old friend. "They're my new band."

Tony laughed, "Fuck off. You're too knackered to play and they are not old enough to know how to."

"No offence taken," Tom sneered.

"I'm sorry. But I know this old bastard is winding me up. Please come inside and sit," Chris's long-haired contemporary offered. The shop smelled strongly of leather and shelves displayed cowboy books in every imaginable colour and texture. Some appeared to be made partly from snakeskin, crocodile, glittering silver leather and even denim. A row of seats on one side was constructed entirely from old guitar amplifiers with cushions on top. There was a small glass-fronted fridge full of chilled Budweiser and three partially empty bottles of different brands of Tequila stood on top. Several guitars were propped in corners, and Danny instinctively picked up a red Stratocaster.

"My customers don't like to be too far from an axe to practice on," Tony said.

"Or show off with," Chris suggested.

Chris explained that bands touring the UK had been stopping off in Leeds to visit Bootleggers for forty years.

"It's an unofficial date on all UK rock tours." Tony reinforced. "I sell them new boots and get backstage passes to all the best gigs in Yorkshire. It's a win-win. So, if these are not your offspring, what's their story."

Chris gave his old friend a synopsis of how they had come to be here and said that they were heading to London to play in a competition.

"Well, apart from him being short, Chinese, and having the haircut of a BBC newsreader, I can't see how you could fail to pass this kid off as Jimi," Tony said, laughing sarcastically.

"Ah, but you haven't heard him play."

Li was seething with anger at what she saw as the disrespect Chris's arrogant friend was showing them. Now, Danny also grew annoyed at being spoken about as though he were not in the room. He remembered reading how Jimi reacted when anyone questioned his talent.

Pointing at the seat under Chris, he asked, "Does that amp work?" Tony turned around and flicked on an electrical switch. An orange light appeared on the battered box, and it buzzed as if confirming readiness. Danny plugged in his own Strat and played one chord to check it was in tune and the volume was up. In the ensuing few minutes, people from all over the shopping centre were drawn to the source of the extraordinary sound. The shop was soon full, as was the mall outside. Other shopkeepers stood outside their doors to hear Danny's impromptu performance. Tony sat in bemused silence, occasionally shaking his head.

"Holy shit. Where the Hell did that come from? That kid is amazing!"

"I told you he was special," said Chris, smirking.

"They," said Li, leaving Chris puzzled.

"You mean 'they' are special. There's three of us in this band."

"Correct. Sorry, Li. They are all exceptional."

Tony gestured for Danny to let him hold his guitar, and he unclipped it and handed it to the older man.

"Nice Strat. Quite old. Sixties?" Danny nodded.

"Listen, dude. I owe you an apology. I should have known Chris wouldn't turn up here with a band that couldn't play, and you are truly outstanding. However, I know a little about this business and, as well as being good, it still helps to look the part. You can't go on stage in London looking like that. You need to walk tall. What size shoe are you?"

Tony began pulling boxes from shelves and throwing them on the floor beside Danny. Chris started opening each one and letting Danny feel the hand-tooled leather. The boots were extraordinary works of art, often with price tags to match. Danny said nothing but seemed fascinated by one pair made in black and silver leather.

"They look like your Strat," Li observed.

"Try them on, mate," Tony urged.

Danny looked at Chris who nodded his assent. When he stood, he wobbled slightly, getting used to the higher heel, but then he rebalanced. Now standing three centimetres taller, Danny appeared more confident and sounded more assertive when he spoke.

"These are cool, but we can't afford them."

Tony whispered something to Chris, who said, "They're yours, Danny, but when we come back to play in Leeds, we get VIP passes for Tony. Deal?"

"Deal," Danny agreed, beaming from ear to ear.

Just then, the lady who owned the vintage clothes shop opposite came over carrying a dark green jacket. "Hi, Tony. Who are your new friends?"

Tony made the introductions. "I heard you play that Jimi Hendrix number and immediately thought you should see this." She handed Tony the braided military jacket. It was a short dress jacket in bottle green, made for an officer of the Hussars.

"Jimi wore a slightly longer version in black, but this has the same vibe. It's been too small for almost everyone who's tried it on. But it might fit you."

Danny shied away, but Li pushed him forward and said, "Just try it, Dan."

The jacket was snug, but it looked great; everyone seemed to agree except Danny.

"We don't know how much it is. And, however much it is, we can't afford it."

"I have had it for ages, and you're the only one who's managed to get it on. I paid fifty quid for it."

Chris interrupted, "Forty quid cash, you say? Sold," holding out his hand for the lady to shake on the deal. "My treat, Danny." Danny looked bemused by all that was going on.

The lady from the vintage clothes shop checked her phone messages. "Before you go, Danny, I think my friend Cheryl, at the hairdressers next door, wants a word."

While all this had been going on, video of him playing and the story of Danny, the band and their trip to London had been circulated by Tony on his social media.

Cheryl came over to Bootleggers from her salon and spoke to the teenagers. "I have no customers for the next ninety minutes. We'll give you all a free London restyle if you can sit down now."

Li answered affirmatively before the two boys had a chance to object and pushed them out of the door and across the mall.

An hour and a half later, Kat and her mum entered the Victoria Quarter just in time to meet the band emerging from Cheryl's salon with their makeovers.

Kat stopped in her tracks and held a hand to her mouth. "What the Hell happened to you?"

Danny looked embarrassed and deflated. "You don't like it?"

"Like it, Danny. I'm in shock. I saw you yesterday. Danny, the geeky sixth-former. In twenty-four hours, you have been transformed into Danny, the rock god. It's... It's just unbelievable. And have you grown taller as well?"

Danny lifted his left leg to reveal his new boots.

"Anyway, you need to talk about transformations. When you dumped me, you were a scruffy hippie with braces on your teeth. You've come back looking like a catwalk model."

Kat now also spotted Li's hair and makeup. "Wow, you look beyond fabulous," and held out her arms for a hug. Li held her hand toward the drummer. "Even Tom's been under the hair dryer and had a beard trim," Li said, laughing.

"Danny, I leave you alone for a few hours and you turn into someone else. Is that jacket like Superman's cloak or Batman's mask - you pull it on and turn into some sort of superhero?"

Danny was relieved. He realised that he only really cared what Kat thought. If she liked his new look, it was cool with him. Chris watched the reunion until Kat's mother came over and introduced herself.

"I'm Alice. Kat's mum."

"Oh, hi. I'm Chris."

"I know who you are. Chris The Lick. I saw you play at Sheffield just before the Millennium. And again, in Glasgow a few weeks later. Then, you came to Middlesbrough, and a friend who worked at the venue got me a backstage pass. You signed my ticket."

"So, are you just a music lover or one of these weird super fans? You don't sneak around emptying the rubbish bins of rock stars hoping to find discarded notes for the next hit song so you can sell them on eBay?"

"Just a fan. Don't worry. Your trash is safe. I thought you were a great guitar player and were very nice to us."

"Ah, that's a shame. Apparently, when you need a lock on your bin, that's when you know you've really made it."

"Well, I thought you were quite handsome in a rugged way."

Chris laughed." A bit of northern rough, you mean?"

Alice joined in laughing. "Jimmy Nail already has that market cornered."

Li came over. "Chris. Would it be OK if Kat and the rest of us had a look around the shops here? There is some amazing stuff here."

"Why not? Alice and I can grab a coffee. It seems we've got some catching up to do. See you back here in an hour."

Chris and Alice each gave a short-hand version of the highs and lows of the intervening two decades –he having lost his ability to play, then lost his wife to Portugal, and she having lost her husband to illness.

Now, it seemed she was losing her daughter to another guitar player.

"Funny how life plays little tricks on you," she summarised.

Raising his eyes, Chris agreed, "I often think someone up there is enjoying a right laugh at us down here."

There was an obvious mutual attraction between the two. Each found the other easy company. They laughed a lot, something neither felt they had done enough of for quite a long time.

"Kat desperately wants to go to London with the band. I have serious reservations and doubt Danny's parents would approve, either."

"What if you came with her? Surely, that would satisfy both your concerns?"

"But how would that be possible?"

"The bus has six births and there would be six of us. You'd just need to go shopping here and pick up anything you need for a two-night trip."

"Gosh, we hardly know each other, and you're asking me to sleep over."

"Yes, on a bus with four teenagers, including your daughter, separated only by curtains."

"You know what – why not? I've been telling myself that I should be more adventurous. Let's do it! Kat will be overjoyed."

When they were all back on the bus, Chris asked, "What do you think about Jimi now that you've talked to people who met him?"

Li looked at the others before answering, "I think we all assumed he was a rebel. A drug-using tough guy you would probably want to avoid, other than when he was onstage."

The others nodded, and Chris concurred, "I think that was most people's view."

"But now I see a quiet, vulnerable guy who had a lot to be angry about but wasn't," Li said with feeling.

Danny added, "People liked him. He was kind to people he'd never met before and didn't flaunt his success or fame."

**CHAPTER TWENTY ONE**

It was early evening when the troupe, now grown to six, drove down a track to a stone farmhouse in Derbyshire. Dogs came rushing from somewhere, barking loudly but with tails wagging. A middle-aged man with long hair emerged from a barn, his arms full of firewood. Chris parked close to him and got off the bus.

"I can't shake your hand until I get rid of these," he said, nodding at the logs.

"Let me take them," Tom offered, stepping forward with his arms outstretched.

When he was unburdened, Chris hugged his old friend warmly.

"Boys and girls, this is Nick. Nick, this is Alice, Li, Kat, Danny, and Tom, you've already met.

Nick writes songs. Good songs. They have been on bestselling albums, and in several films and TV series."

"No, I write music," he corrected. "My wife Eva writes lyrics. That's why we're still together after twenty-five years. We're useless alone and can't make a living without each other."

"So, you're not a farmer," Li asked.

"Well, I'm a musician first, and I play at being a farmer when the real work is done. Music pays for the farm's losses, is what my wife says."

"That's the opposite way around to most wanna-be musicians who need proper jobs to pay for their guitar hobbies," Chris added, slightly cynically.

Nick led them all inside the farmhouse, dogs trailing at their heels. Inside, it smelled of baking bread. "Eva's baking focaccia to have with our supper."

"It smells delicious," Tom said, sniffing the air with the enthusiasm of a teenager who had not eaten for hours.

Nick explained that they had invited their neighbours over for supper. There would be too many to eat at their kitchen table. So, as it was a fine, dry night, they were going to BBQ and eat outside.

"So, you can all help Eva carry stuff out. As you've already got the wood, Tom, you can get the fire going. Bring plenty more logs, it tends to get cool up here later."

Everyone was allocated a job and got on with it. Danny seemed reluctant to lose sight of the bus because his precious Strat was still onboard. Chris suggested he bring the guitar and take it to the house where Eva was cooking, and he seemed happy with the idea.

Sally and Mike arrived from the smallholding next door. Sally had brought a tray, which she explained were foil-wrapped bananas with rum and raisins to bake on the fire later. Mike carried a six-pack of beer and a bottle of Champagne.

"The perfect guests," Eva said.

A feast followed, which included two whole chickens. These had been stuffed with herbs and garlic, wholly encased in bread dough and baked in an outside wood oven.

"Those are two of the cockerels you've been complaining about waking you at 5.30."

"In that case, I shall enjoy them even more," Mike joked.

Tom brought more logs and the fires roared with the new fuel, then talk turned to music. Nick raised his glass for a toast. "To Chris and his success as a songwriter at long last." Although they joined in the toast, Sally and Mike looked to them for an explanation for the congratulations, which Chris was happy to supply.

"Ah, yes, there's no substitute for owning copyright," Mike said, addressing the teenagers. "Right now, it probably seems great just getting on stage and playing, but at some point, you need to get creative or go and get a proper job."

Now, it was their turn to look puzzled. "Creative?" Li questioned.

"Playing covers is fine, but that music is someone else's intellectual property, which they should be paid for. Like Chris will be from now on, with his song in the movie. If it becomes a Christmas favourite..."

"Oh, yes, please!" Chris interjected.

"Chris is entitled to be paid for his song every time it is performed. Remember the song Love Is All Around You, from Four Weddings and a Funeral? That song was written by Reg Presley in 1967. Twenty-five years later, it became a huge hit again on the back of the film. Even though the recorded version in the film was by Wet Wet Wet, the songwriter still owns his rights to royalties."

Chris, who had been listening carefully, said, "Now I finally have something worth leaving; I think it's time I made a will, to stop my wife from getting her hands on my songs. I would turn in my grave if I died and then had another Love Is All Around You-type hit, and she got all the money."

There was a pause in the conversation during which the crackling fires were the only sounds. Then Li said quietly, "I have some songs."

Everyone looked surprised, but Danny looked shocked.

"You've written songs? You never said."

"I don't know if they are any good. Also, I can't sing," Li said shyly.

"Kat sings like an Angel," her mum proclaimed with great pride.

"Muuuum," Kat protested.

"But it's true. She sang really well in school performances but even better in her bedroom. She's got some recordings on her phone."

This was Danny's queue to be shocked for the second time in the evening. "You never said anything about singing," he said, looking hurt.

"Like Li, I didn't believe I was any good."

"Mike strode off, quickly returning with two acoustic guitars, and handed one to Li."

"Let's hear your favourite song. I presume you wrote down the lyrics?"

Li told everyone she had the words on her phone but was embarrassed about sharing them.

"People write to express their feelings and, the more personal they are, the better the song. But who really understands the lyrics to any song?" Sally contributed. "Fans have speculated about the meaning of famous songs since time immemorial, but only the songwriter knows for sure what they meant."

"WhatsApp me the words, Li," Kat said. "I'll try to sing along with you if that helps."

Li started nervously with a chord progression on Mike's expensive acoustic guitar, which sounded much better than anything she had ever played. Her lyrics were barely audible until she got to the chorus, which was quite a simple yet clever play on words.

Mike interrupted, "Now that we have the tempo and the chorus, why don't you start from the beginning? We will try and join in where we can."

So, it was that the world premiere of Li Chen-Curran's debut song was performed around a campfire in Derbyshire. Mike added a simple backing on his other guitar, and Tom produced a basic beat with his hands on the table. Kat joined in the lyrics with some confidence, causing her mother to smile and appearing to send a shiver through Danny. Sally and Eva broke into spontaneous but quiet applause during the first chorus.

"Boys and girls, I think you now have a proper band," Mike exclaimed.

"Complete with a songwriter," Nick added, looking pleased with himself for having coaxed Li into sharing her talent.

**CHAPTER TWENTY-TWO**

On the following day, the bus made its way slowly through the London traffic, as they spotted signposts to famous landmarks and shouted familiar street names such as, "Look, Harley Street!"

A little further, "Coming up on the left, Baker Street – in 1967 the site of the ill-fated Apple Boutique, The Beatles first venture into non-musical commercial activity, which lasted less than a year,"

Chris added.

"Baker Street was also the home of Sherlock Holmes, as well as the title of the song with the most famous saxophone solo in pop. A pound for anyone who can name the singer," he challenged.

"Gerry Rafferty," Alice quickly answered.

"An extra pound for the chart-topping band he formed."

Alice looked as though she had to think for a moment and then shouted, "Stealers Wheel."

They continued through the ever-busier traffic. "We will soon pass Grosvenor Square, the site of the former US Embassy. In 1968, this was the scene of a riotous anti-Vietnam war protest attended by which famous band's frontman and was allegedly the inspiration for one of their hit songs?"

After a short silence, Chris answered, "Mick Jagger and the song was Street Fighting Man."

"Really. I didn't know that was what that song was about. Makes sense, I suppose." Alice mused.

"Now, as we reach Saville Row, you'll need to look up to see where The Beatles played their legendary final live performance on the roof of Apple Records HQ."

They all craned their heads upwards, although there was nothing much to see.

"And finally, here it is, everyone," Chris announced. "The famous Bag O Nails. The venue for Jimi's first proper live show in the UK, attended by everyone who was anyone in British rock and pop, at that time. It's still pretty much as it was back then. Now it's a private club but available to hire."

"That would be a great place for us to play at," Danny suggested, only half joking.

"Where Paul McCartney met Linda Eastman," Li announced, having just learned the anecdote from Wikipedia.

"It would be quicker to note the artists who didn't come here during those halcyon days of the sixties than to list those who did. Even those musicians who never played here came to see other bands. But it held less than a hundred people. On some nights, you might be standing shoulder to shoulder with a lineup of pop legends that could easily have included all the members of The Beatles, The Rolling Stones, The Who, Cream and so on. And, as all of them were not famous faces then, you might not even have known who they were."

**CHAPTER TWENTY THREE**

When it came to the final live performance in front of an invited audience, Danny was suddenly overwhelmed by uncertainty and insecurity. He forced himself to put on the Strat, fasten the strap, then stare into space for a moment. With tears welling in his eyes, Danny turned to Li and told her he was sorry, but he could not go through with it. Packing his guitar back into its careworn case, he was shaking with fear. Kat hugged him from behind, but he refused to be pacified. Then Li had an idea.

"Danny, you know you will be fine as soon as you play. You always are. Do you remember those videos we found of Jimi playing with his back to the audience at huge concerts? In an interview, he revealed that he didn't always like showing his feelings on stage. That he wanted private moments with his thoughts and just the feedback from the amplifier, even in front of thousands of people."

Danny nodded, recalling the image Li was referring to. Jimi had looked so lonely for a man at the peak of his career surrounded by people who adored him.

"Why don't you let us go on stage and set up without you," Li proposed. "You plug in one of those long cables we brought from the tour bus but stay offstage. When I prompt you, play the first chords of *Hey Joe* before walking on as we join in. It is also a different opening that might make us stand out. We know that Jimi was shy in real life but was not afraid to become a performer when he got on stage."

Billy and Jing had gone backstage to wish their two children good luck. Billy held open his arms for a group hug. This time, it was LI's turn to say, "Come on, Danny. It's us against the world." But the prospect of their group chant did not work its magic. Danny was not smiling as he usually did. His face was expressionless as he mumbled something.

"What's that, Danny?" his father asked.

"I can't do it, Dad," he said quietly.

"You can." his father reassured him.

Now, almost shouting and on the verge of crying, "I'm not Jimi. I'm just Danny with a second-hand guitar and an old jacket. That doesn't make me a star."

Chris was beginning to think he would not see his prodigy achieve his moment in the spotlight, and get one more roll of the dice for himself through him.

"When Jimi first stepped onto that stage in London, he was unknown, oddly dressed, and black, playing to an audience who mostly all knew each other, all shopped in Carnaby Street, and were white. Britain already had its own guitar hero in Eric Clapton, people sprayed 'Clapton is God' on walls, and he wasn't alone. People like Peter Green, Jeff Beck and Jimmy Page were also pushing on behind him, all of them taking black music and making it their own, and making waves, while Jimi was still nobody. He was a stranger in a strange land, an outsider with few friends and only his talent to speak for him. You are no more a fish out of water than he was, and he blew them all away. You can do the same. Do it for Jimi. Do it for me. Most of all, do it for yourself!"

The event MC came over, followed by the judges, so they could be introduced to the bands. Jimi's former girlfriend, Lucinda, now in her late seventies, smiled kindly at Danny, almost as though she recognised him from somewhere.

A bell rang, indicating the show was about to begin, and everyone started hurrying to take their places.

Lucinda turned away and walked back past Danny. She hesitated and gave him a quizzical look. He turned his head toward where his father was watching, as if he might have some explanation. He looked as nonplussed as Danny and by the time he turned back, she was gone.

**CHAPTER TWENTY FOUR**

As Li had planned, the band were on stage without Danny when he played the first hauntingly familiar chords of *Hey Joe*. Danny stepped out into the waiting spotlight just as Tom hit his first drumbeat. But this was not the shy, tearful teenager of a few moments earlier. Standing tall in his new boots, looking more relaxed in his green coat and with a half-smile, Danny had morphed into another being. Li and Tom were slightly surprised but elated. He nodded to them as if to say that all was well, and this gave them the confidence to up their own game.

By the time it came to the first solo, the audience and judges were wowed by the band's show. Chris was speechless as he witnessed the best live performance of Jimi's classic song he had ever seen. "He looks like he's been taken over by the spirit of Jimi himself," he said to Alice.

"Maybe he has," was her simple reply.

Billy was in tears – partly of joy but also of trepidation about what was to come.

## Hope the Dude Can Play

By the end of the first song, the audience was on their feet, clapping and cheering. The judges were trying to maintain an air of impartiality, but Lucinda's enthusiasm was hard to disguise, and it was infecting her colleagues. Somehow, Danny managed to seamlessly move into the next song, All Along the Watchtower, without a break. Tom and Li had to think quickly to keep up, but they did.

They had been expecting *Wild Thing* to come next, but just as the last chord of Watchtower faded away, Danny covered his microphone with his hand and turned to Li and Tom. "Voodoo Child," he enunciated. Save *Wild Thing* for the encore. I've got a good feeling about this, trust me."

By now almost all of the audience were on their feet, and so were two of the judges, Lucinda included.

It had been Tom's suggestion to finish with *Wild Thing* when they had been deciding what songs they were going to play, but Danny had disagreed. He liked the reassuring order that came from following the same setlist. With just a fifteen-minute slot they simply did not have time to get through all the songs they usually played. Li agreed with Tom that it was too important not to play their best songs. The ones they knew their audience liked the most. "Then we should play the first three, or the last three but in the normal order," Danny had argued, his need for consistency in his life overriding the logic of his bandmates. He had been adamant.

They had been told that only the winners would get to play one extra song once the decision was announced. What had caused Danny, to skip their strongest number midway through the most important performance of their lives, left them puzzled.

When all the competing bands had played, the MC returned to the stage to thank them. There were messages from the sponsors for him to read out and then he had to deploy his comedy routine to fill in for ten minutes while the judges made their decision. The audience was still groaning from his first joke - "What's the difference between a guitar player and a large pizza? A large pizza can feed a family of four" – when a woman came on from the side of the stage and handed him a gold envelope. Danny, his band, Kat and his parents were all huddled together heads down and arms around each other's backs. Chris had turned away, as if afraid to watch their reaction.

"And the winner is..." the MC imitated a drum roll with his hands. "Spirit of Jimi!"

When all the clapping, cheering, and whistling died down sufficiently for him to be heard, the MC welcomed Danny and his band back for an encore.

"Oh shit," Tom said.

"What's the matter?" Li asked wearing a huge grin. "I didn't expect to need them again, so I gave my drumsticks to that pretty girl in the front row who was smiling at me."

"What! Who do you think you are, Mitch Mitchell?" Chris handed him a spare pair he had brought with him along with extra plectrums and guitar strings, just in case.

"Forever the pro," Danny said, putting his arm around Chris, and looking thankful.

The judges came to offer their own congratulations. "That was amazing, Danny. I shut my eyes when you were playing, and it was as if Jimi had been brought back to life. It is quite extraordinary." Lucinda said, looking emotional. "Can I take a closer look at your guitar, Danny?

He reluctantly handed the Stratocaster over.

"It's exactly like the first one Jimi had when he arrived in London. He used to sit in our flat and practice for hours every day. Someone else famously said, there were three of us in that relationship. In my case, my competition for his attention was his guitar."

Lucinda turned it over, scrutinising it closely before handing it back. "Thank you. It is a real sixties classic. From your accent, you are from the North?"

"Darlington", Danny answered shyly. They chatted for a while, with Lucinda asking questions and doing most of the talking. Already nervous about the event, he was also in awe of being in the company of one of his hero's friends.

Danny was relieved when she asked, "Is that your father over there watching us?"

Danny nodded, and Lucinda walked over to speak to him. The fear in Billy's eyes confirmed all she asked about that guitar's provenance.

## Hope the Dude Can Play

The MC ushered everyone off stage to let the band play their encore. "I think we all know what to play," Danny announced. They all nodded.

"But how did you know to save this song?" Tom asked.

Danny shook his head as if he didn't believe what he was about to say. "The guitar told me."

"What?" Li exclaimed. "Now I know you are completely crazy."

"I know it sounds weird, but I just get a feeling from it of what to play. I can't explain it any better than that. After the first two numbers, I got the sensation that Voodoo Child should come next. I was not even thinking about an encore."

His bandmates shook their heads in disbelief and prepared to play their final number.

Using one of the pedals they had been loaned by Chris's mate, along with their tour bus, the opening note was stretched out and distorted to make several seconds of screaming guitar. Then Li's bass added the rhythm that kicked off the song. Tom thought it was a very different opening to The Troggs version, but he knew that to many of their usual audience, this was the first time they had heard any of these songs.

They were just great songs, played well, in a different style to anything they had heard before, without comparing them to the originals. Their context was the one they were in now. Even the supporters who had come along to support the other bands were loving it: clapping and cheering and dancing in the aisles.

**CHAPTER TWENTY FIVE**

At the side of the stage, Lucinda chatted to Danny.

"Your son is on the spectrum, isn't he?" Lucinda said to Billy's surprise and great relief. He had been sure she would ask how he had come by the guitar. Glad of this diversion, he confirmed he was, adding, "I only recently discovered that I am as well. But how did you know, if you don't mind my asking?"

"My brother George was autistic and had a similar, extraordinary musical ability. He has enjoyed a brilliant and rewarding career working for recording studios, mostly on classical recordings. He can spot one bum note from a single violin in a forty-piece orchestra. Your son can copy Jimi's playing so note and tone perfectly, I doubt even a computer could tell them apart."

"I can only hope my son enjoys a fraction of your brother's success," Billy answered, wondering where this conversation was going but happy that it was not where he had expected. Then it suddenly changed direction.

"And you're from Darlington?"

Billy nodded confirmation.

Smiling kindly, she continued, "And Danny plays a sixties Strat, similar to the one Jimi misplaced in Darlington in the winter of 1967?" That drew another nod from the embarrassed Billy, only this time his head stayed bowed. He was dreading what he knew was coming.

Billy then realised that there was no point in continuing to play games. "OK. How do you know? There were hundreds of black Strats in circulation back then. What makes you so sure this is that one Jimi lost?"

Adding to Billy's discomfort, she said. "I am the only person alive who can, without question, identify the guitar that went missing that night."

"As far as I know, there was nothing unique about the Strat Jimi lost. It had no special features when it left the factory, and as far as anyone knows, he did nothing to change it. It would be impossible to identify with any certainty," Billy countered, knowing that he must have sounded defensive.

"So, you've been doing your homework. But why would you do that?"

Billy was beginning to get angry at the thought of what this would do to his vulnerable son. "My boy loves that guitar. It has become his entire life, just like it was for Jimi. It looked like it might have been stolen again recently from their rehearsal room, and Danny just went to pieces."

"It was nearly lost again, you say? How ironic. But obviously, you got it back." There was a pause. Now sure she knew the truth; Lucinda adopted a more conciliatory tone. "The special feature I'm referring to was not added at the factory but in our flat in London."

Lucinda told the story of how Jimi had been out one night and left her alone in their tiny flat, getting ready for an upcoming weekend of parties. She wanted to varnish her nails, but Jimi's paraphernalia covered every flat service. "He was like a magpie for collecting junk," she explained. Turning Jimi's Strat upside down on the sofa made it a passable surface on which to balance a bottle of black cherry polish from Biba.

"I still wear the same colour, although no longer from Biba", she added, waving the fingers of her right hand.

Lucinda went on to tell how the bottle had tipped over, spilling the nail varnish onto the guitar's black paintwork.

"I managed to wipe it off the surface, but some had run into the edges of the backplate." It wasn't especially noticeable because the colour was so dark. Jimi never mentioned anything and so I got away with it."

Billy began to understand the potential consequences of the revelation that Jimi's guitar was easily identifiable.

"I've just examined the join around the backplate of Danny's guitar and there are still signs of that dark nail varnish around the plate. Like Jimi, Biba is long gone, but that varnish was literally as hard as nails."

Billy looked crestfallen. The secret he had kept for nearly forty years looked as if it had been uncovered. His exposure would surely mean the end of the road for Dannys's band and any chance of a career in music. He might even now be arrested for theft. He had checked, and there was no statute of limitations on crimes in the UK. He would be as guilty now as back in 1967.

Lucinda paused before asking, "Tell me how you came to have the guitar. The truth, mind you. No bullshit stories about winning it playing cards in a pub."

Billy told Lucinda the whole story. All the memories of Jimi flooded back and brought tears to her eyes. In her memory, she could also replay her brother's struggles with his autism and imagine what Danny had overcome to get up on stage here today.

"OK. So, you didn't steal it so much, as you found it in the street but failed to report that fact to anyone."

"So, what do you intend to do now?" Billy asked, expecting the worst.

"What I remember from that night in Darlington is that I had gone outside through the fire exit of the venue to smoke a cigarette. You were already there, having had too much to drink, vomiting into the gutter. Some younger local louts who had been thrown out of the gig started leering at me in my mini skirt and being rude. They were also making racist remarks about Jimi.

You recovered yourself and came to my defence, bravely chasing them off."

Billy's face remained emotionless because he had no idea what fiction was coming next.

Lucinda continued, "We then chatted for a while before Jimi came out. I told him what had happened and what you said about wanting to play guitar. But also, that you would never be able to afford one on your wages.

"That very week, Chas had bought Jimi a new white Strat to celebrate *Hey Joe* getting into the Top Ten. So, he now had three almost identical guitars, just in different colours. He simply handed the black one he was carrying to you as a thank-you for coming to our aid. He was famously generous. I gave you a hug and a kiss and we went back inside where Jimi said, "By the time we come back to Darlington, I hope that dude can play."

Lucinda winked at Billy conspiratorially. "No theft was reported to the police that night because nothing was taken. Someone must have witnessed a slightly drunk teenage boy running away from a Jimi Hendrix gig carrying nothing but a guitar and a big grin. They just assumed the worst. The rumour mill took over, and the legend of the lost Darlington Stratocaster began."

Billy absorbed this story with puzzled amazement but was unable to see how he could possibly contradict it without enormous repercussions. Lucinda advised that they agree to keep this story a secret. Otherwise, there was a risk of huge publicity, which would doubtless result in all manner of spurious claims over the now highly valuable guitar.

She raised her right index finger with its black cherry nail varnish to her lips, indicating a sealing of their shared secret.

On stage, the band reached the climax of *Wild Thing,* and the audience went crazy. In a blaze of feedback, Danny held the Stratocaster high above his head letting the note fade, like Jimi used to do.

Billy's face suddenly went ashen with fear. "Oh my God. He's not going to trash that guitar into the amp like Jimi did, is he?"

Lucinda shook her head calmly. "Just let the dude play."

THE END

## Acknowledgements

One of the most enjoyable aspects of becoming an author is the fascinating people that one encounters during research. No one more so than Bob Smeaton, who has been enormously generous with his time and advice in the creation of this novella. It turns out that our paths had been moving in concentric circles for thirty-plus years and were only very recently nudged into the same orbit by serendipity. As the director of several of the definitive documentaries about Jimi, one of which earned him a Grammy, there was simply no one better to contribute than Bob. One of his skills is to view a story through a cinematic lens, where action does not necessarily follow a linear path and several events can be taking place at once in different locations. Without his input, this would undoubtedly be a poorer story.

Mike Brough has done his usual magic trick in creating a stunning cover without any real brief, with limited resources and little time. We were aided considerably with the cover challenge by the kind assistance of journalist Chris Lloyd and the agreement of his employers, *The Northern Echo* in allowing use of their photograph of Jimi.

Several other people made contributions to my knowledge and understanding of the events that led to this story for which I am extremely grateful. These include:

Ian Martin
Mike Prendergast
Ian & Carolyn Emerson
Ian Luck
Simon Cassidy

My apologies to anyone who added to my knowledge that I have forgotten to include.

*~James Vasey*

*James Vasey*
*Photographed in Seborga*
*2020 by Kaidi-Katariin Knox*

**James Vasey**

A former magazine editor, entrepreneur and university lecturer, James is now an author dividing his time between the North of England and Liguria in Italy.

It was his discovery of the ancient Italian village of Seborga, its historical connection to the Knights Templar, its unique culture and the traditional cuisine that was the inspiration for his first book, Cooking up a Country in 2017.

A follow-up, Unlikely Pairings arrived in 2020. A third book, Recipe For A Nation, in what has become the Seborga Series was published in 2021. A keen interest in artisan food and wine, as well as environmental issues, is reflected in James's writing.

An international coalition has ambitions for a feature film based on Cooking up a Country and has been working towards that end since 2021.

As well as this Jimi Hendrix story, more recently James has been working on a foodie detective series, as well as an illustrated children's storybook entitled The Dog In The Wrong Place. It is hoped these works will see the light of day during 2024.

Thank you for reading Hope the Dude Can Play.

If you liked the story

please consider leaving a review on

Amazon.com

Goodreads.com

Or other online venues.

For updates on books by James Vasey, follow:

www.facebook.com/jamesvaseyauthor

Printed in Great Britain
by Amazon